End of

Cowboy Rough Book Three

By

Darah Lace

This is a work of fiction. Names, characters, places, and incidents are either the product of the author's imagination or are used fictitiously, and any resemblance to actual persons living or dead, business establishments, events, or locales, is entirely coincidental.

End of His Rope ~ Copyright 2022 by Darah Lace

All rights reserved. No part of this book may be used or reproduced in any manner whatsoever without written permission of the author except in the case of brief quotations embodied in critical articles or reviews.

Cover Art by Diana Carlile
http://www.designingdiana.blogspot.com

Published in the United States of America

Praise for

Darah Lace

SEXTING TEXAS

"I am a HUGE sucker for a friends to lovers trope and this one was a really good one. I loved this story. Both characters want the same thing, but are terrified of ruining their friendship… Texas is shy…but Will definitely knows how to push her buttons. They know each other so well… It makes this story work so well!"

~Christie, Smitten with Reading

BACHELOR AUCTION

"The characterization in *Bachelor Auction,* complete with the wealth of emotion Ms. Lace weaves with language left me completely absorbed, I could barely tear my eyes away. More than that, the slow, steady journey on which Marcus and Charlotte embark leads to sizzling chemistry and complete, utter satisfaction with the conclusion. Do not, do not, do not miss this book."

~Denise, Happily Ever After Reviews

BUCKING HARD

"Darah Lace made a fan of me with her fabulous book, *Bachelor Auction,* and I've been keeping an eye out for more of her work ever since. In this short, sweet story, we're introduced to tomboy Bradi Kincaid, a little girl no more, and pining as always after her best friend, Mason Montgomery. Since coming home, Mason has taken a healthy notice of Bradi, as well…and he doesn't exactly know how to reconcile the fact that his childhood chum developed a woman's body."

~Lynn Marie, Denise's Review

Chapter One

Evan McNamara rolled to his back, his body spent. The mattress dipped as Clay made room to settle Lindsey between them. Her soft sigh of sated contentment whispered across his shoulder, and a familiar and unwanted irritation surged within him. He should have been content. Long hours of sexual play with the two people he cared for and trusted most had become an oasis from a week of monotony. He loved the time they shared with him. Loved being a part of their threesome.

But lately…

He swung his legs over the side of the bed, sat up, and rubbed a hand over his face.

Gentle fingers trailed over his arm. "Where are you going?"

Capturing Lindsey's hand, he twisted to kiss her palm. Light from the midnight sky sifted through the blinds, tinting her long blonde hair and tanned complexion a pale blue. "Some of us have to work tomorrow."

"It's Saturday." She yawned, garbling the last half of her words.

He smiled and checked the face of his watch. "No, sweetheart, it's twelve-twenty a.m. *Friday*. You've got your days mixed up."

She patted the mattress beside her. "You should get some sleep before you head out."

Clay looked up from where he nuzzled the curve of her neck. "Give it up, Lindz. You should know by now he's not sleeping over. He never sleeps with subs."

No, he didn't. Couldn't. Not even Lindsey. Especially not Lindsey. She belonged to Clay. Even if she didn't, sleeping with a sub meant intimacy, and he hadn't done intimate since leaving home nine years ago.

"I have a lot of work to do before I leave Sunday." It was true and as good an excuse as any.

His brother Josh, older by two and a half years, wasn't the kind to ask for help, but with a broken arm and leg, he hadn't had much choice. Evan was part owner of the family ranch southeast of Austin. If anyone was going to take over running it while Josh healed, it should be him.

"At least stay for breakfast." Her words slurred with her need for sleep. "I'll make your favorite chocolate chip pancakes."

"Those are *your* favorite." He placed her hand on the pillow beside her angelic face and stood.

The restlessness clawing at him had nothing to do with work or the trip ahead of him.

In the bathroom, he stripped off the condom, tossed it in the wastebasket, and turned on the shower, hoping to wash away the agitation that had him feeling like one of the caged cougars he and Josh had trapped in the canyon back home.

Home. He hadn't been there in too long, wouldn't be going back now if not for Josh's injuries. Evan had built a career as an attorney with a prestigious Houston law firm, accumulated material things for convenience and comfort, and played at Silver House, the fetish club where he'd met Clay. They'd clicked at once, both Doms who liked to share a submissive female, to watch as the other brought controlled pleasure—or pain—to their play.

They'd taken turns as lead Dom until three months ago when Lindsey reentered his friend's life. Clay would never allow it, and Evan would never dream of insisting. He'd known from the beginning the two had feelings for each other. He was simply their third.

Maybe that was his problem. He'd gone too long without complete control of a scene. Not that Evan begrudged them their happiness. They were in love, engaged to be married. But he could feel the dark hunger rising inside him, and as much as he tried to ignore it, he wanted more, needed more.

He stepped into the shower, shut the door, and leaned into the hot spray. Hell, maybe being home would help clear his head. If he knew Josh, busted up or not, he'd shout orders from the rocker on the porch and keep him busy from dawn to dusk until only a hot meal and a soft bed mattered.

God knew Stone Creek had nothing else to offer. Not anymore.

****

Everything Shayna Webber had ever wanted was coming to Stone Creek.

Well, not everything, but definitely one of the top ten on her wish list. Somewhere between a vacation in Scotland and winning the lottery, she wanted Evan McNamara. To be precise, sex with Evan McNamara. Again.

Okay, maybe he was at the *top* of her list. He was that good.

She'd had him once, and over the last nine years, she'd dreamed of him often. More than often. Every time she'd had sex, in fact. In the aftermath of a so-so orgasm, her thoughts would drift to Evan and the fiery passion they'd shared that one night, and she'd ached for the bone-melting, universe-altering orgasm that remained elusive ever since.

And now his brother Josh was handing her the opportunity to make it happen.

"So have you given it some thought?" he asked.

A twinge of panic mixed with excitement tugged at her belly. She turned from Josh's semi-naked form. One cast from his toes clear to his upper left thigh and another from his fingers to just above the left elbow hardly qualified as clothing. Nor did the sheet strategically placed to hide his man parts.

She soaked the washcloth she'd been bathing him with in water from the basin on the makeshift nightstand. "Yes, I'm just not sure yet."

Josh had sprung the news on her yesterday and needed her answer before she left this morning for her weekend shift at the hospital in Austin. Evan was taking a leave of absence and would be here when she returned on Monday. That meant living in the same house with him, eating at the same table, breathing the same air.

"I'd understand if you didn't want to come back," Josh said. "I wouldn't have asked him for help if I didn't need it. The guys know how to keep things running, but they can't make the tough decisions."

"I know."

The ranch hands had run in and out of the house, constantly waking Josh when he tried to rest, agitating him because he couldn't fix whatever was wrong the way he wanted it fixed.

He was a lot like his brother in that way, demanding control of everyone and every situation.

They looked alike, too. When she'd come across Josh in the emergency room, her heart had jumped. She'd thought he was Evan and almost turned tail and run. But then he'd smiled that crooked, cocky Josh smile, and her racing pulse had slowed to just a hair above normal.

Josh had always been a little rough around the edges where Evan was smoother, more polished, prettier. Actually, Evan was beautiful.

That hadn't changed if the pictures on the mantel told the truth. He'd filled out a bit and, if possible, grown sexier. His shoulders were wider, his hair a bit shorter, probably to fit his lawyer image. But his eyes remained the steady, focused, piercing sky blue that, even in the photo, made her skin hot and her panties damp.

He'd been an important part of her last summer in Stone Creek. Her all-consuming everything. They'd been inseparable. And in love.

Or so she'd thought.

Shayna set the bowl and cloth aside, squirted moisturizing cream into one palm and rubbed her hands briskly, warming the lotion. With care for Josh's comfort, she crawled to the middle of the bed and motioned for him to sit up and face the other direction. When she'd first arrived, Josh was sleeping on the sofa because he couldn't climb the stairs, and due to no full bath on the bottom floor, he smelled. She'd immediately had the ranch hands move his king-size bed into the den downstairs and given him a sponge bath.

Josh braced his upper body on his good arm and wrestled to get upright and comfortable. "Damn, I hate being laid up." He shot her a quick once over. "Especially with a beautiful woman in my bed."

"Yeah, yeah, you'd rather be getting laid than be laid up. I've heard that one before."

A low chuckle preceded a grunt of pain as he finally found a position that seemed to suit with both legs draped over the edge of the bed.

"Comfy?" She waited for his nod, then began massaging his back. His shoulders were broad, brown from the early summer sun. If he hadn't been hurt, his skin would be darker now that the warm days of June had faded into the scorching heat of July.

The tight muscles in his neck eased under her practiced thumbs, and he lowered his chin to his chest with a moan. She was good at her job, but working with a body like Josh's was more pleasure than toil.

Having been without a man too long, there were moments she'd considered letting him take their playful flirtation to another level. But they'd been smart enough not to cross that line years ago and to do it now, when things were about to get really complicated…

Her stomach flipped for the hundredth time since Josh had told her Evan was coming home. Nine years was a long time and a lot had happened. She had changed. She was sure he had, too. He was a hotshot tax attorney, had made partner last year. Wasn't married. Josh had told her that. But he probably had women falling at his feet in some highfalutin' country club.

The last time she'd seen Evan, she'd been a naïve nineteen-year-old country girl with limited knowledge of sex and even less experience. He'd been worldly to her—twenty-two and a college grad on summer break with law school on the horizon.

"I don't know what I'd have done without you these last couple of weeks." Josh shifted to lay a hand on her jean-clad knee, drawing her attention back to blue eyes a shade darker than Evan's. His mouth tipped into a teasing grin. "And I'll never find someone as pretty to look at. Probably get stuck with some old bat who won't let me feel her up."

Some of her anxiety fled as she pictured Josh trying to flirt with Nurse Hadley in the ER where she worked. The woman ran the place with an iron fist. He'd be so miserable when she ran off all his lovely visitors. "Then I guess I can't leave you stranded."

"Really?" The sincerity of his relief wore down the last of Shayna's indecision.

Still, she rolled her eyes and feigned a weary sigh. "Someone has to make a sacrifice. Might as well be me."

Silence settled over the room while she continued to massage lotion into Josh's arm and leg. Thoughts of how she'd get through the next few weeks with Evan in the house had her stomach in knots.

And her feminine parts warming.

All he'd ever had to do was look at her and her insides melted. One touch had her panting. And kiss? God, that boy could kiss. With the brush of his tongue, he could make everything around her disappear. Including her clothes. And the one time they'd had sex…freakin' hot. She'd never been able to find that again.

But that would all change if her plan worked.

When Josh told her that Evan was coming, she'd almost packed up and left. But after she calmed down and took a moment to consider what seeing him could mean, she couldn't think of anything else. From there, a plan had developed into a hair-brained scheme to seduce him into a sex-with-no-strings fling.

It wasn't so much that she wanted closure. She'd been as much to blame as he had for what happened that night. But she would sure welcome knowing how he could leave without a word—not even a text. He'd just dumped her like yesterday's leftovers. No, this plan was about fulfilling nearly a decade of fantasies.

The fantasies had developed over the years, starting out as a small wistful thought after sex with her first lover since Evan. It hadn't gone well. With each unremarkable orgasm, the fantasy had blossomed. She'd dreamed of having someone take her as he had, longed to feel her lover's punishing fingers dig into her flesh or tangle in her hair, to have him pound her pussy without restraint. No one had ever made her come so hard that she existed only on another plane.

A little shiver shook her at the memory of the not-so-gentle way Evan had taken her against the cool hard ground. Of the delicious bruises the next morning—

"You okay?" Josh's deep raspy voice woke her to the fact she'd stopped massaging.

She set her hands in motion, trying to shutter her mind from the erotic images. "Yeah, sure. I'm fine."

She wasn't about to tell him how hard her nipples were, how her belly swirled, and her clit throbbed. God, she wanted Evan. Wanted him bad, bad, bad.

But would he want her?

No, she wouldn't think about him rejecting her again. The first time had hurt enough to put her off men—and sex—for a couple of years. But she'd been in love with him then. This time would be different.

She wasn't looking for forever. She just wanted a repeat of what he'd given her before, a pleasure so sweet it was almost painful. Or was it the other way around? Either way, it had been a fan-freakin'-tastic orgasm, and she merely wanted to explore the urges Evan had awakened in her all those years ago. Urges she'd never been able to fulfill with any other man.

At twenty-eight, she should have been able to ask for what she wanted. And she'd tried a few times. The first attempt had begun with an eager partner but ended in disappointment. The last one had scared the shit out of her, and she hadn't asked again. Two partners in between had looked at her as if she were depraved.

Hell, she probably was. She only hoped Evan hadn't changed and was still just a little on the twisted side, too.

Chapter Two

Stone Creek had more to offer than Evan thought.

From the top of the ladder leaning against the barn, he watched the brunette getting out of the small sedan at the back of the house. She certainly offered an enticing view. Tall, slender, legs that stretched for miles. Thick, wavy hair, long enough to ensure a good grip, and a firm, heart-shaped ass that invited a man to hang on tight and enjoy a hard ride.

His gaze followed the swing of her hips across the yard and up the porch steps. As the screen door banged shut behind her, he lost the mouth-watering vision. Another one of Josh's buckle bunnies. No less than four had been by to check on him since Evan arrived last night.

This one, though, seemed more at home than the others. She hadn't knocked, just walked on in as if she had the right.

Screwdriver in hand, he went back to the broken hinge that needed replacing. Only time would tell whether she was "the one" Josh had hinted about over dinner. While Josh was known for his charm, he didn't encourage women to linger. Probably had a schedule to keep them from running into each other.

Twenty minutes later, Evan descended the ladder, his curiosity getting the better of him. This one obviously had Josh's interest. The others hadn't stayed as long.

Evan dropped the screwdriver in the tool chest and looked back toward the house. Maybe he should let them have their privacy. If she was "the one," they might not take kindly to an interruption. And with the restlessness he hadn't been able to work off, he didn't need the added stimulation of bouncing bedsprings.

Taking his time, he stowed the ladder and tools in the shed, then turned his mind to finishing the list of chores Josh had written down so he wouldn't forget. As if nine years away from the ranch could erase the previous twenty. His dad wouldn't have allowed him to forget. One chore forgotten always lead to several more to right those left undone.

"Mr. McNamara?" Cal Jessup, one of the three ranch hands, ambled into the barn from the corral. A young, wiry, and somewhat jittery cowboy, he worked hard but didn't seem to have much confidence. He made up for it in loyalty.

"What are you still doing here?" He'd watched Rusty and Mark pull out an hour ago.

He'd assumed Cal had, too.

"I exercised Star. Do you need anything else?"

"No." Evan grabbed the broken bridle Josh wanted fixed and moved the stool near the door into the shade. "You can head on home."

"Thanks." Cal shifted from one foot to the other, rotating his hat by the brim at his waist. "Kylie's been texting me nonstop for the last hour. Wants to show me her costume for tomorrow's dance recital since I can't be there. It's her first."

Evan sat down, hooked the heel of one boot on the bottom rung, stretched the other in front of him, and glanced from the frayed leather to Cal. "Why can't you be there?"

Cal's face scrunched up. "I dunno. I guess I just never thought about asking off."

He pushed his hat back on his forehead. "A man should be there for his daughter's first recital. Don't you think?"

A big grin split the cowboy's face. "Yeah, yeah, I do. Thanks, Mr. McNamara."

"It's Evan."

Cal nodded. "Evan."

The man's gait had a lighter hitch to it as he sauntered off, and Evan frowned. He'd have to talk to Josh about being more in tune with his employees. All of them had lives outside this ranch. His brother certainly didn't have a problem living his.

He cast a glance at the house, wondering how much longer he should wait. His stomach was gnawing on his backbone. Of course, it wasn't going to appreciate the peanut butter and jelly sandwich he forced on it. He didn't cook much other than a simple breakfast, and Josh had been living off sandwiches since his accident. Maybe the brunette could cook.

The sun had gone behind the trees when Evan let himself in the back door. He hung his hat on the hook to the right, and the aroma of baking bread filled his nostrils. Ha! She *can* cook. Probably why Josh hadn't shooed her off as quickly as the others.

With a hot meal to look forward to, Evan was eager to get cleaned up. He trod quietly through the kitchen and into the hall. Soft feminine laughter made him pause at the bottom of the stairs, one hand on the newel post. He'd heard that laugh before. Years ago. A laugh that whispered across his skin, awakening every nerve.

With a slight lean toward the living room, he could just make out the long slender legs and shapely ass of the woman he suspected would knock his world off its axis. He let go of the post and stepped into the room for a better look.

His brother sat on his bed, shirtless, jeans with one leg cut off to accommodate the cast and the fly unzipped, his hair wet and slicked back. The mystery woman—not such a mystery anymore—straddled his good leg, her upper body hovering over Josh's, so close her breasts jiggled precariously near his brother's face.

Fire blazed in Evan's gut as memories of another time and a similar situation filtered through his mind. Memories that had haunted him until he'd given into them and faced the truth of who and what he was.

"Watch out, darlin'." Josh's hand, the one not encased in a cast, landed on her outer thigh and slid up the seam of her jeans to settle on her ass. "Though I don't reckon I'd mind if you fell in my lap."

She slapped his hand away but laughed again as she angled his head to one side and even closer to her breasts. Her nipples were hard and poking through the thin, pink T-shirt. "Settle down, or I'll tie you to this chair."

"Promises, promises." Josh tugged at a damp curl at her temple. "You're all wet."

"Occupational hazard." She threaded her fingers through his hair. "Now, be still. I need to make sure your skull is intact."

Josh's gaze flickered Evan's way, and a grin split his face. "Hey, Ev, look who I found."

Evan stepped around the couch. "I see."

What he saw was Shayna Webber. His "the

one." Not Josh's.

His chest tightened, and his heartbeat accelerated at the sight of her half draped across his brother. She looked good. Better than good. She looked damn sensational. And not at all a girl anymore. She was all woman. Question was, had she become Josh's?

He shook off the thought. He had no right to wonder, much less have an opinion. Resting against the arm of the couch, he attempted polite conversation. "How are you, Shayna?"

"I'd be a lot better if your brother would behave long enough for me to check his stitches." She didn't bother to look up from her examination of Josh's scalp.

"I found Shayna in the emergency room when the boys took me in." Josh winced as she dabbed what looked like iodine on his head. "I talked her into taking care of me on her days off."

She looked over her shoulder at Evan, her full lips pulled into a smirk. "He hired me for home healthcare services."

Evan's stomach clenched as those dark eyes flitted over him and back to his brother.

"Hey, I tried talking you into other services."

"A sponge bath and dinner are all you're getting." Shayna straightened and scooted back to gather a first aid kit and towel Evan hadn't noticed on the coffee table. "Besides, the shape you're in, you couldn't handle much servicing." She slid her gaze to Evan again, this time meeting his head-on without a hint of what she was thinking. "Good to see you again, Evan."

She glided from the room, the scent of soap and vanilla lingering in her wake. He resisted the urge to sniff the air or, worse, trail after her like a hound with his tongue hanging out.

"Who knew nurses could be that hot?"

Ignoring his brother, Evan sank onto the couch. "You might have mentioned Shayna was the home health professional you hired."

"Didn't want to spoil the surprise." His brother chuckled as he reached for the towel on the bed and tossed it in a basket in the corner. "And just think, I might have missed seeing her if I'd put off fixing the roof one more day. She only works weekends at the hospital."

Evan tried to remember what Josh had said about the nurse he hired. She worked weekends at a hospital in Austin but took occasional odd jobs during the week to supplement her income. She lived in Austin but would be staying the week in Stone Creek. Here. In the same house. Sleeping in Josh's old room, just next to his. The two of them alone up there.

What the hell difference did it make where she slept? Though she claimed otherwise, she might be with Josh now. Besides, he'd blown his chance with her nine years ago. Blown it all to fuck.

"You gonna eat?" Josh tried to maneuver on a crutch through the maze of furniture. "She cooks like a dream."

Evan's stomach growled, reminding him he was hungry. But another part of him was hungrier, a part he couldn't feed. That didn't stop him from rising and running a hand over his hair to smooth out the hat creases. "Yeah, smells good."

Josh nodded. "Right behind you. Just gotta put a shirt on."

Without waiting to see if Josh needed help, Evan wandered down the hall to the kitchen. He stalled against the doorframe, suddenly not knowing where to stand or what to say. She seemed unaware of his presence while his body raged with so many emotions he couldn't figure out which one to focus on first. He didn't even try.

Better to see which way the wind blew. Taking a fortifying breath, he readied himself for the worst. Then again, it had been a long time and maybe she'd forgotten all about him and what he'd done to her. And maybe he'd grow wings and a halo. "It's good to see you, too, Shay."

A slight pause as she reached for the biscuit pan was the only indication she'd heard him or even realized he was in the vicinity. She shut the oven door, turned it off, and set the biscuits on the stovetop. "Supper's ready."

It was odd to see her in a domestic capacity, her actions precise and efficient as she fussed about, adding spoons to the bowls of steaming food and gathering condiments from the fridge. Everything smelled good, but he couldn't take his eyes off her to check out what his growling stomach told him to get busy eating.

"If you'll put the food away when you're done," she said, moving the salt and pepper from the stove to the table, "I'll clean up in the morning."

His gaze flew from her hands to her face. "You're not eating?"

"I'm coming off a fifty-six-hour shift." She wiped her hands on a dishtowel, then draped it over the back of a chair. "I'm about to crater."

Disappointed but more than a little relieved, he turned sideways to let her by. But instead of brushing past him, she stopped in the doorway and laid a hand on his chest. His stomach clenched, and his heart slammed against his ribs.

"I promised myself," she said as she rose on her tiptoes and leaned against him, "if I ever saw you again…"

Her other hand wound around his neck, and her gaze fell to his lips as she closed the space between them. He sucked in a breath, catching the vanilla scent that never failed to make him think of her. His dick swelled behind the fly of his jeans.

In the next heartbeat, her mouth met his, and her body, warm and supple, melted against him. Shock and uncertainty ricocheted through him, lust hot on their tail. He didn't know why she'd want to kiss him after what he'd done, and he still wasn't sure if she was Josh's "the one," but fuck if he cared. He wanted the kiss, wanted what it would lead to if she were willing.

His first instinct was to take control, but when her tongue flicked his bottom lip, he curled his fingers into fists at his sides to keep from hauling her closer. He'd lost control with her once and wouldn't make that mistake again. He hadn't known what he was back then, hadn't known how to control his needs.

Instead, he opened for her, allowing her to explore at her own pace. Unlike her kisses when they first met, she wasn't shy about her exploration. The kiss took him back to the time near the end, after he'd taught her what he liked and how to please him.

Her tongue danced around his, drawing him out, luring him into the hot cavern of her mouth. She sucked him deeper, her cheeks contracting around his tongue. His cock jerked at the first slow pull, and heat pooled in his balls.

The suction on his tongue eased, and the fingers at his neck slipped away. Her teeth nipped his lower lip. "Goodnight, Evan."

Her slight weight lifted, and Evan opened his eyes as she turned and strolled down the hall, passing Josh, who, by his expression, had obviously seen the kiss. They both watched her round the newel post and trot up the stairs.

Josh gave a low whistle and wobbled closer. He didn't look pissed or hurt, so maybe they weren't a thing. "And here I thought the two of you parted in a bad way."

Evan blew out a long breath and wandered into the kitchen. He slumped into the nearest chair. "We did."

"Guess she's not holding a grudge." Josh settled across from him and handed him a plate.

"Guess not." Every now and then, he'd thought about how it would play out if they ever met again. He'd expected the silent treatment, for her to pretend she'd forgotten him. Mostly, he figured there'd be some yelling, though Shayna hadn't been a yeller. But he'd have welcomed a few pots and pans thrown at his head.

Not once had he ever imagined she'd kiss him like that. As if nine years hadn't separated them, as if it were only yesterday they'd made out under the willow by the lake. As if he hadn't taken her virginity in a careless manner, out of control with both jealousy and lust, then left town the next morning without a word.

"Looked like an invitation to me."

Lost in thought, Evan barely heard Josh's words spoken around a mouthful of buttered biscuit. An invitation? His dick jumped, ready to RSVP.

"All I know is—" Josh swallowed and took a drink of iced tea. "—if I got an invitation like that, I wouldn't be sitting here with your sorry ass."

Normally, Evan wouldn't either. He was accustomed to going after what he wanted. But something he hadn't felt in a long time crept up his spine and kept his *sorry ass* stuck in the chair. He'd like to think he knew better than to try to relive the past. But that wasn't it. He'd like nothing more than to have Shayna in his bed, to make up for how he'd treated her before, to use what he'd learned over the years and give her the pleasure he'd denied her back then. Just the thought of her bound and gagged…

Fear. Plain and simple fear. And guilt. God, the guilt. What if he lost control again? Hurt her again? Shayna had a way of pushing his buttons like no other woman could or had since. Worse, she'd learn what he'd become. He wouldn't be satisfied with vanilla sex, not with her, and he couldn't look in those big brown eyes and see her disgust. No, better just to steer clear for the next few days. She'd be gone again Friday.

Granted, she'd be back Monday, but maybe

he'd sneak a trip home this weekend, go to the club Saturday night and scout out a new partner. Tate Albrand came to mind. They'd worked well together a few times. They'd pick out a new sub and play all night. Smooth out the edge of this gnawing need inside him.

Yep, he could stay busy and away from Shayna.

He gave a mental nod and reached for a biscuit. "Think I'll ride fence tomorrow."

"Send Mark. I need you here tomorrow."

"Mark's on his way to Dallas."

Josh's fork stopped halfway to his mouth. "What for?"

"He's proposing to his girl."

"Guess you talked him into that. He's been holding on to that ring, scared shitless to pop the question."

Evan shrugged. "The boy just needed some encouragement."

A grunt gave way to silence as they both dug into the baked chicken on their plates. Evan didn't like asparagus in general, but this wasn't bad. He'd have preferred fried chicken and mashed potatoes, but being a nurse, Shayna probably kept more to a healthy diet for her patients.

Josh waved his fork at Evan. "Cal can check the fences."

"Cal's daughter has a recital."

"Dammit, Ev. We're teasing the new mare, and Rusty might need your help. I can't do it."

No way in hell was he sticking around to watch a horny stallion prance and sniff around some mare's rear end. He was in enough trouble with the little filly upstairs swishing her tail. And damn, she swished good. "I don't know enough about horse breeding to be of any help. I'd only be in the way."

"You can lead a horse, can't you?" Josh took another bite of biscuit and chewed around his words. "'Sides, this would be a good time to learn. You do own half this ranch."

"Yeah, and you can learn tax law while we're at it." Evan pushed his chair back and took his plate to the sink. "We've got a good system going. Why screw it up?" He rinsed the plate and put it in the dishwasher along with the fork and his glass. "You should think about giving Rusty a raise. Heard he got an offer from Bellamy."

Josh sat up straight. "Who told you that?"

"Mark."

"You're not here twenty-four hours, and you're already in everyone's business, solving their problems." Josh pointed his fork at Evan. "You do that so you don't have to think about your own." He pointed upstairs.

"What?" He feigned innocence. "I don't have

any problems." At least he wouldn't after a quick trip to Silver House. "She works for you."

"But she kissed *you*." Was that an accusation? "Which is why you're making excuses to run off."

"Hmm, and here I thought it was because I'm doing you a favor." Evan pushed his chair in and headed for the back door. Josh knew him too well and was hitting too close to home with more than a few truths. "It is on your list. You know, the one that's a mile long. Or don't you want my help?"

The warm night air hit him square-on like a wall of heat as Josh got in the last words. "You are so full of shit, Ev. Full. Of. Shit."

****

Grabbing his boots, Evan left his room and crept down the hall. His plan to get out of the house before dawn, before Shayna got up, had failed.

With only a thin wall separating his bed from hers, images of her lying there naked had taunted him, not to mention the confusion her kiss caused. Sleep had eluded him until the wee hours of the morning. He'd woken to sounds of her moving around in her room. His only chance was to sneak past her door without the floorboards creaking.

He sidestepped the one that got him in trouble more times than not when sneaking in late at night. One more just outside her door and…

A low hum came from the other side of the

paneled wood. Not a hum, a buzz. What the hell? She couldn't be doing what he thought she was doing.

He groaned as an image of her pale skin against dark sheets filled his head. Silky hair splayed around her head like a decadent veil, one hand plucking at rosy nipples, her slender legs bent and spread wide as the nimble fingers of her other hand worked the buzzing vibrator over her pouting clit. His cock thickened, and his balls tingled.

Shit, he had to go.

Instead, he stepped closer to the door and winced as the cranky floorboard he'd meant to avoid complained beneath his weight. The door swung wide, and Shayna stood there with an electric toothbrush in her mouth, white foam around her lips. Her head tilted to one side, and a single dark brow lifted.

"I—" Speech denied him as he took in the buttercup sundress with strings holding it up and a hem that hit her mid-thigh. The buttons at the neckline were undone, showing off the creamy cleavage bound in a pink lace bra. And damn if he couldn't smell her powdery scent. She was too close.

She held up one finger, brushed past him, and padded ten feet to the bathroom at the top of the landing. Gathering her hair, she bent and spit in the sink. He should have been making his exit while she rinsed, but the dress lifted in the back, not high enough to reveal anything more than leg, but he'd always loved those long sleek satiny—

Evan shook himself mentally. He wasn't some peach-faced boy who'd never seen a woman before. He was one of the most sought-after Doms at Silver House. Yet here she was, making him feel like a stammering virgin.

Get your ass moving, man.

The glue on his feet finally gave, and he took the stairs two at a time. At the bottom, he shoved his feet into his boots. Her footsteps on the stairs lit a fire under his butt, and in five strides, he was in the kitchen.

"Mornin'." Josh already sat at the table, coffee cup in hand.

"Mornin'." Evan skirted his brother, snatched a baggie from the cabinet, and stuffed it with leftover biscuits. "I'm heading out."

Shayna sashayed into the kitchen and opened the refrigerator, blocking his path to the back door. "Don't you want breakfast?"

"No, I'm good." He zipped the baggie as she shut the door and placed a carton of eggs on the counter beside him.

Again, he remembered the cougar in the canyon. How the male cat had paced the wall behind him until instinct forced him to fight for his life. Josh had gotten too close to the frightened cat before Evan could take the shot and still had the scars to prove it. Intentional or not, Shayna was backing Evan into a corner, and he'd left her with too many scars already. He wouldn't add to them.

"I'll have lunch ready at noon."

"Don't bother on my account. I won't be back 'til late." He backtracked around the table, aware of Josh's amused gaze following him. Grabbing his hat from the hook, he blasted out the back door, screen slamming, to safety.

****

Shayna had yet to put her plan in motion, except for last night's kiss, and already, she'd hit a stumbling block. How was she going to seduce Evan if he wasn't around? She'd wanted to take it slow, to flirt and build the sexual tension. She wanted to make him so hot and horny that he'd fuck her fast and hard against the wall or over the kitchen table.

Looked like she was going to have to kick it into high gear and make every second count.

Arms loaded with excuses to follow him, Shayna backed through the screen door and headed for the barn. The violet glow of the rising sun barely lit the backyard. The barn was dark, but a soft whinny gave her direction, and she found Evan in the corral behind the barn. He looked up as she approached but immediately turned his attention back to the saddle.

"I brought you some water." She dodged a pile of horse manure and squeezed in between him and the fence. "If you're going to be out all day in the heat, you'll dehydrate."

He hesitated, then took the bottles she handed him and stowed them in the saddlebag. "Thanks."

"A couple of oranges for energy, and a banana for potassium."

His gaze landed on the fruit she clutched against her chest, and for a second, she thought she saw a flicker of heat. But his eyes were clear of any interest when they shifted to her face.

"Thanks," he repeated and held out his hand.

The fruit went in the bag with the water, and suddenly, Evan was climbing on his horse. The moment was slipping away.

Do something.

She grabbed his thigh above the knee and looked up at him. "Hey."

His leg tensed, and the animal beneath him shifted. He pulled lightly on the reins and glanced down at her with the stoic patience she remembered so well. Damn him. Her heart pounded like a hundred horses stampeding across her chest, and he sat there with no reaction at all.

She shoved aside a rise of uncertainty and

trailed her fingers slowly down his calf. "I'm making baked salmon and steamed veggies for supper." She let her gaze drift to his mouth. "What would you like for dessert?"

Me, me, say me.

"Whatever Josh wants." He nudged the horse forward and forced Shayna to step back. Without another word, he kicked the horse into a trot.

"And what if Josh wants *me*? Would you want me then?" The hushed words, unheard by their intended target, struck a chord deep within her core. Her pussy clenched and her breasts grew heavy at the memory of how he'd played voyeur that night with her and Tucker, encouraging her with his eyes. Would he enjoy watching her with Josh?

No, she wouldn't use a friend to gain a lover. Besides, a best friend was one thing. His brother was a whole other matter. Evan's reaction to her advances so far wasn't very encouraging, and defeat was exhausting, not at all good for morale.

Shoulders slumped, she made her way back through the barn to the house. She couldn't do any more to further her plan until tonight anyway. Josh was still waiting on breakfast, and she had laundry to wash.

As she walked in the back door, Josh's head popped up, his gaze scanning her face. "Didn't go well, huh?"

Grabbing a bowl from the cabinet and the egg carton, she pretended not to understand his question. How could he know what she was doing anyway? "What didn't go well?"

"Your attempt to seduce my brother."

The egg she'd been about to break dropped on the counter and cracked open. With a heavy sigh, she tore a paper towel from the roll and began wiping up the mess, trying to ignore the sinking sensation in her stomach. If she was that obvious to Josh, that meant Evan knew what she was doing, too. And avoiding her was his way of dealing with it. "Yeah, well, he's not interested."

"Bullshit." The vehemence in his voice surprised her.

She turned to face him, a little hopeful he knew something she didn't. "You think he's interested?"

"I know he is." His lips turned up in a crooked grin. "That was one helluva kiss you laid on him last night. Kept me up for hours, and I was only a bystander."

She turned back to the eggs, a hot blush seeping into her cheeks. She still couldn't believe she'd done it. Kissing Evan within the first ten minutes of seeing him again hadn't been part of the plan. But before she'd even realized what she was doing, she had her tongue in his mouth as if it were the most natural thing in the world. As if she had every right to do so. As if her heart wasn't beating a mile a minute and her knees weren't threatening to send her to the floor.

But it wasn't just the kiss that had her skin sizzling. The picture on the mantel was nothing compared to the real man. The way his long frame had eaten up the doorway, crowding her into the small kitchen. Golden waves, crimped where his hat had been, made her ache to feel it against her breasts, her thighs. Oddly, the dust of a hard day's work on bronzed skin only added to his masculine appeal. And his scent? A faint hint of citrus from his morning cologne, the slightest tang of sweat, and a mix of fresh hay and leather.

And then there was the thick swell of his cock against her belly.

She bit back a moan and pressed her legs together to quell the ache. Her vibrator—only for use if he said no, along with a box of condoms if he said yes—waited in the nightstand upstairs. She could take the edge off after breakfast, but now that she'd kissed him, nothing artificial would do. She couldn't give up yet.

"'Course, I remember what it feels like to be on the other end of one of your kisses."

The heat in her face flamed higher, and the whisk in her hand beat faster. "You're incorrigible."

"You love me that way."

She exhaled a mock sigh of resignation. "Guilty as charged."

And she did love him in a good friend kind of way. He'd been there for her after Evan left that summer.

Growing up, she'd never really thought of Josh. He was older than Evan, didn't party with her friends much. He'd been busy running the ranch, the mostly unseen older brother she'd planned to get to know when Evan married her. But Josh had found her at the lake the week after Evan abandoned her, when she'd finally realized he wasn't going to call.

At first, she'd been afraid of Josh when he'd ridden up and asked what she was doing. It was private property, and as far as she knew, he didn't know her from Adam. But then he'd plopped down in the grass beside her, teased her into a smile, then told her he'd listen if she needed to talk. She'd burst into tears and let him hold her until there were no tears left to cry.

When she'd looked up at him, he looked so much like Evan. The need to feel Evan's lips against hers one more time had pushed her to close the distance between them. Josh had accepted her kiss and, for a moment, kissed her back. Then he'd broken the connection and reminded her he wasn't Evan.

After that, they'd become friends, sometimes

meeting by the lake. She often thought their friendship might have developed into something more if her family hadn't moved to Austin. All Shayna knew was, she owed Josh for more than giving her this job.

Turning around, she said, "Thanks for being there for me when I needed a friend."

She expected a flippant answer, but he stared at her for a full minute then frowned. "I have a confession to make."

The seriousness in his voice made her wary, and she wasn't sure she wanted to hear him out. She didn't want the easy way between them to become awkward. "What is it?"

"I had ulterior motives for hanging around you back then."

Oh god, here it comes. Please don't tell me you had feelings for me. "What was that?"

"I needed to know what happened with you and Ev."

Whew! Wait, what? "I don't understand."

"Whatever it was put him in a bad way, and he wouldn't tell me anything. I couldn't fix him if I didn't know what was wrong. Course, you never would tell me either, and he threw himself into school and ignored my offer to listen."

That didn't make sense. She was the one who got dumped. Why would Evan have been upset?

"The night you guys had your fight," Josh continued as if reading her mind, "or whatever it was, I found him in his room. At first, I thought he was drunk. He was just sitting on his bed, holding his head. But when he looked up at me, I could tell he'd been crying, and he looked scared. I thought someone had died. Then he flew into a tizzy, started packing his bags, telling me to explain to Mom and Dad that he had to get back to school early for something or other." He waved a hand at her. "Wasn't 'til I saw you that day by the lake that I knew the problem was with you."

"And you thought I'd tell you?"

"Yeah, but you were as tight-lipped as he was. I tried keeping him informed about how you were doing, but he shut me out. Wouldn't talk to me for a long time after. Not until Mom's funeral a few years later."

Josh had done the same for Shayna, giving her tidbits of information about Evan. She'd gobbled them up.

"Then you moved, and I lost track..."

She leaned a hip against the counter. "Why are you telling me all this now?"

"Because he's never been the same since, and I can tell you still have wounds that haven't healed. I know you still have feelings for him."

"What? No, that's not what this is about at all."

"You keep telling yourself that, but I see the way you look at his pictures when you think I'm not watching. And how you look at him now."

She shook her head. "It's not like that. I just want…"

"Sex?" He laughed. "Whatever you say. But I'm telling you now, Evan ran nine years ago and he's running now. Which says it all because my brother doesn't shy away from something he wants. Trust me, he wants you. So, whatever happened between you two, *you* have to be the one to get it out of the way."

Chapter Three

Food put away, dishes done, and laundry started, Shayna left the house to think about what Josh said. A shaded bench near the neglected flowerbed beckoned. Flowers of all colors had once framed the house, and she'd sat there many an afternoon that summer, waiting for Evan to finish his chores. The wood needed a coat of paint, but it was still sturdy as she plopped onto it and closed her eyes, letting the morning breeze cool her cheeks.

How was she supposed to "get it out of the way" when she didn't know what *it* was? Well, she knew what happened, but *after*… That was what she wasn't sure about.

He'd been quiet driving her home, but he was always quiet. No matter how many times she turned it over in her head, the only thing she'd ever come up with was that they'd finally had sex. And he hadn't wanted to.

All summer she'd ached for him to make love to her. From the second she'd seen him at Toni Willis' graduation party, Shayna had fallen hard. They'd spent every minute of free time together after that, and she'd been sure he'd fallen, too. Kissing had led to groping, which had progressed to oral sex both ways, but as much as she begged, even in the most heated moments of passion, he held strong, refusing to accept the gift of her virginity.

Until that night…

The three of them, Shayna, Evan, and his best friend from high school, Tucker, were the only ones still at the lake after a long day of swimming and partying with friends. Someone had lit a campfire, and the flames cast provocative shadows under the canopy of the willow. She was tipsy from too much wine, Tucker was three sheets to the wind, and Evan… She could never tell with him, but he seemed a tad more mellow than usual.

A chill skittered over her sun-pinkened skin as the wind picked up, and she wished for more than the bikini and shorts. Waiting for Evan to return from nature's call to keep her warm, she idly spun one of the empty beer bottles.

"Ha, now you have to kiss me." Tucker sat up, weaving a little and presenting his puckered lips.

"Are you trying to steal my girl?" Evan appeared from the other side of the low-hanging limbs. He'd left with a bare chest and swim trunks but returned wearing a T-shirt.

Tucker, on the other hand remained shirtless, his chest sunburned except where the light sprinkle of dark hair protected his skin, leaving it blotchy pink and white. He pointed to the beer bottle. "She spun the bottle, and it landed on me."

Evan laughed and settled next to Shayna. He gathered her onto his lap, arms wrapped tight around her. "What do you say, Shay? Wanna kiss that ugly mug?"

Giggling, she kissed her finger and tapped it on Tucker's nose. "There."

"My turn." Evan leaned into her to reach the bottle, and she nearly toppled from his lap. He caught her with another easy laugh and gave the longneck a spin. It landed with the tip toward them. "I get a real kiss."

His mouth slanted over hers, and she opened for him, accepting his tongue with equal fervor. His hand moved over her back as the kiss deepened. She hummed and arched into his body.

"Jesus, you guys make me hot." Tucker's voice broke through the haze of lust, and she pushed at Evan's shoulder.

Evan pulled back, his eyes dilated to nearly black, only a slice of blue surrounding his pupils. "Hot doesn't begin to cover it."

"Your turn, Shayna," Tucker insisted.

Dragging her gaze from Evan's beautiful face, she twirled the bottle. It landed on Tucker.

"Yeah, baby!" Once again, he leaned forward, then paused mid-way and backed up. His head shook like a dog trying to get dry after a bath. "No fingers. I get a real one."

She smiled at his demand and, without leaving the warmth of Evan's lap, braced herself on one hand to reach Tucker's face. He puckered up, but she twisted to the side and gave him a peck on the cheek.

"Awe, man, this game sucks."

And so the game went. More alcohol was consumed, a newly emptied bottle replacing the old. When Tucker spun the bottle or if she spun and it landed on Tucker, he received a peck on the cheek. When Evan spun and it landed on her, or vice versa, a long make-out session ensued.

Five or six rounds into the game, Tucker's turn came up and he refused to spin. With his elbow on his knee and his chin in his hand, he mumbled, "What's the point if all I get is a stingy peck on the cheek and you guys get foreplay?" An exaggerated sigh whooshed from his lungs. "I wish Julie was still here 'cause I'm drunk enough and horny enough to make a move."

"Oh, poor baby. Do you feel left out?" Laughing, Shayna crawled from Evan's lap to kneel next to Tucker and patted his cheek. "I'm sorry. Let me make it better." She rained tiny kisses all over his face, several landing on his lips. "Does that make up for it?"

He grunted. "Maybe a few more."

She shot a quick look at Evan, winked at his lazy smile, and plastered Tucker with another round of kisses. The third time, when she zeroed in for a smack on his lips, his hand captured the back of her head and held her there for an open-mouthed kiss.

Stunned at the invasion of his tongue and with the

delayed reaction of intoxication, she didn't pull away. The kiss wasn't unpleasant. Maybe a bit wetter than Evan's but not one of those slobbery ones either. Then she remembered that she shouldn't be analyzing another man's kiss with Evan looking on and backed out of the kiss. She blinked at Evan to check his reaction, afraid he'd be mad.

Light from the fire made it easy to read the emotions flitting across his face. Surprise then jealousy, but they were fleeting before his features settled into acceptance, eyes blazing with lust, his full lips parted for the quick inhale and exhale that expanded his chest. He wanted her to kiss Tucker.

Through a dull fog of alcohol-induced confusion, she'd looked at Tucker and her breath caught at the sexual tug in her belly. Funny, she'd never noticed how attractive he was. Dark hair and eyes, muscles on muscles, and an easy personality. Probably why he and Evan were friends.

Shayna lifted her gaze to Evan's once more, and her own emotions catapulted from hurt and uncertainty to desire. The hunger in his eyes fed her need to please her man.

Slowly, her gaze locked on Evan, she lowered her mouth to Tucker's, brushing her lips against his. Evan's eyes narrowed on their lips, encouraging her to deepen the kiss. She met Tucker's tongue in the brief space between their lips, and all three of them moaned.

Tucker took over from there, drawing her with him as he lay back on the ground, her half on top of him.

Another glance at Evan shot a jolt from her nipples to her pussy. Or maybe it was the way his eyes followed the path of Tucker's hand near her breast. Her body hummed as she realized she held the power to Evan's pleasure. All summer he'd controlled their time together, deciding how far they'd go, giving her orgasms with his mouth and fingers but refusing her need for deeper penetration.

More drunk off power than wine now, she put everything she had into the kiss, sucking Tucker's tongue into her mouth to imitate the slow fuck Evan denied her. Tucker's thumb grazed her nipple through her bikini top, heat zipped to her core, and suddenly it wasn't just about Evan watching. Tucker knew what he was doing and did it well.

That thought scared her a little even as she tilted her pussy to rub against his muscular thigh. But when his big hands cupped her ass and he ground his hard cock into her hip, she realized she had to stay focused. The kissing was fine but to have Tucker touch her in places only Evan's hands had been…

She could still give Evan a show if that's what he wanted, one he'd never forget. She simply had to change direction, which meant taking the power from Tucker, too.

Breaking the kiss, she trekked wet kisses along his neck, down to his chest. Every few inches, she peeked Evan's way. The increasing speed of his breathing and the heated glint in his eyes sent a rush of wetness to drench her bikini bottoms and bolster her courage to continue her path lower.

On her knees between Tucker's legs, she followed the grooves of his six-pack until her mouth found the top of his treasure trail. She paused, waiting for either of them to stop her. When only the sound of their breathing reached her ears, she slipped her fingers under the elastic waistband of his swim trunks and tugged.

"Oh, yeah," Tucker breathed as he lifted his hips and shoved his shorts down. His stiff cock sprang free, veins bulging through the taut skin on his shaft, the head dark and shiny with pre-cum.

Licking her lips, she wrapped her fingers around the wide base then hesitated. She checked for Evan's approval. His eyes blazed hotter, and his hand covered the crotch of his swimsuit. Her tummy did a little somersault, and the wetness between her legs soaked through to her shorts.

He wanted her to suck Tucker's dick, wanted to watch.

And she'd let him.

Shayna didn't regret it. Blowing Tucker in front of Evan was one of the hottest things she'd ever done. And then he'd finally given in to whatever was holding him back. He'd fucked her hard and good. So good.

He'd been quiet afterward. Again, nothing new. When he took her home that night, he'd said he would call and kissed her briefly on the lips. That was the last time she'd seen him until yesterday. And she was no closer to figuring out what she'd done to make him bolt now than she had been back then. The only thing she could do was offer a vague apology and hope for the best.

That and make sure he understood she wasn't looking for a relationship, just an earth-shattering orgasm.

****

Darkness greeted Evan as he walked into the kitchen. He stopped at the sink to wash up, then ventured down the hall toward the study. He'd checked the figures Sunday afternoon when he arrived, but he needed the calming effect of numbers. They helped him focus and took his mind off whatever—or whoever—was bothering him.

The television blared from the den, so he paused in the doorway. Josh was parked in the recliner in front of the TV.

"Fence is down by the lake," Evan said. "I'll fix it tomorrow."

Josh reached for the remote and lowered the volume. "You went by the lake?"

"How else would I know the fence is down?"

His brother shrugged. "Just surprised is all since you two"—he waved a finger from Evan to the stairs behind him—"used to make out there and you're doing your damnedest to avoid her."

Evan glanced over his shoulder, certain she was there, listening. Relief made his head swim.

No one there.

"She's taking a shower. You're safe."

"I'm not avoiding her." He turned away and walked across the foyer to the study.

"Liar," Josh called out.

Evan didn't know why he bothered to deny the truth from Josh. His brother was the only person he'd ever talked to about his feelings for Shayna. But that had been before he left. Later, he'd been too ashamed to confess the particulars of their breakup. Josh would have kicked his ass from here to next Sunday.

After flipping on the light, Evan crossed the room and eased into the chair behind the desk. It had been a while since he'd ridden. Longer since he'd been on horseback all day. He'd be sore tomorrow.

He opened the ledger on the computer and scanned the spreadsheet Josh had emailed him last month, then flipped to the one that showed income and expenses for the current month. The ranch was solvent, more so than most outfits in the area. Times had been tough, but Josh had a keen instinct for ranching, as had their dad.

Evan's gaze swung to the family picture on the wall to his left. He and Josh were still in high school when it was taken, the last one with their mom and dad. She had passed from a brain aneurism a few years after he left for law school, their dad two years ago after getting hung up between a bull and a fence.

"Josh is all tucked in."

His head snapped toward the door. Shayna leaned against the frame as if she planned to make camp there. He nodded and turned back to the computer screen, hoping she'd take the hint and go away.

"I can heat up your dinner. It's in the fridge."

"Thanks, but no." The numbers on the screen blurred as he struggled not to look at her. If he did, he wouldn't be able to stop.

"Good, then we can talk."

Talk? He didn't want to talk. They had nothing to talk about that didn't involve the past, and he didn't want to go there. The only thing they had in common now was his brother. "Is Josh okay?"

"He's fine. Got a little cabin fever maybe."

Straightening from the doorjamb, she strolled toward him and around the desk, forcing him to give her his attention. She planted her barely covered ass on the desk, her legs dangling over the edge, her calf brushing the arm of his chair.

Close, too close. Always too damn close. And never close enough. The temptation was almost too much. He sat back in his chair to put some distance between them, which gave him a really good view of the visual feast she presented. He could handle it, though, if she didn't stay too long. Besides, he could allow himself that much.

Her long sable hair was nearly black, still wet from a shower. A navy-blue T-shirt clung to her breasts, the lack of a bra obvious with her dime-size nipples prodding the soft cotton. Her cut-off jeans were short and rode low on her hips so that her bellybutton ring winked at him, teasing him with the reminder of how he'd once dipped his tongue into that shallow well for a taste of her sweetness. There and a few inches south.

His mouth watered, and he could almost taste her honey.

"I owe you an apology."

Her soft murmur drew his gaze to her face, but he barely registered the words as he zeroed in on the soft fullness of her mouth. A mouth that had touched his only last night. Was that why she apologized?

"It was only a kiss." One he'd never forget. One he wanted to repeat.

"No, not for the kiss." A smile tilted one corner of those lush pink lips. "I'm not sorry for that. I enjoyed every second of it."

So had he. Which was dangerous since he'd thought of little else today, trying to figure out what it meant, mostly reliving it, expanding it into fantasies that made him ache to touch her now. To slide his hands up those smooth creamy thighs and grip her sweet ass. He'd pull her onto his lap or bend her over the damn desk.

"I promised myself," she rambled on, oblivious to the swelling of his cock, "if I ever had the chance, I'd absolutely kiss that hot mouth of yours."

Jesus, she hadn't changed at all, still blurting out whatever crossed her mind. He dared not think about what else wandered through that intricate, over-thinking brain.

"Actually, I wanted to apologize for what happened nine years ago."

He might as well have jumped in the lake mid-winter. Cold filled his veins, and his heart almost stopped. His erection deflated, and his balls sagged.

"We don't have to talk about that." He didn't want to relive it. He'd done his best to block the memory.

"Yes, we do." She scooted off the desk and began to pace. "It's haunted me for years."

Haunted her? Tangled hair a mess around her pale face, tears welling in those puffy red eyes... He'd never been able to exorcise that ghostly image. "We were young and stupid. And you're not the one who should apologize. I am."

"Is that how you remember it? As stupid?" She stopped in front of the desk, hands on her hips.

"We didn't use a condom." *Really? That's the best you can do?*

She smiled. "Okay, that was pretty stupid. And we got lucky."

Yes, they had. He'd worried incessantly during the weeks that followed that she might be pregnant. When Josh rattled on about her, he waited for the news. But it never came, and he'd stopped listening.

"I hurt you, Shayna." Finally, the admission he'd held inside for too long found release. "I could have hurt you a lot worse. I was out of control."

Her head tilted to one side for a minute, then she smiled. "You *didn't* hurt me though. Well, I ached in places I didn't know existed the next morning, but Evan..." Leaning over the desk, she planted her palms on the smooth maple, breasts jiggling. Her eyes brightened, partly with a giddy excitement, partly with desire. "It was the best sex of my life."

He blinked. What the hell did she just say? He couldn't have heard her right. Best sex? Of her life? Were they talking about the same night?

His face must have revealed his shock because hers crumpled. "Oh, so it wasn't good for you." She pushed off the desk, wilted into one of the guest chairs, and stared at the floor. "Funny, I never considered that you didn't like it. I should have, though. You kept saying no."

She sounded sad, as if he'd just popped her pink birthday balloon. Yet he didn't have a clue what to say. That night had changed his life forever, awakened cravings he hadn't understood. Cravings that scared the hell out of him but wouldn't let him be until he'd had no choice but to figure out how to satisfy them without hurting someone the way he'd hurt Shayna.

Her shoulders lifted and fell on a heavy sigh. "And here I thought we could spend the time we're here…"

Spend their time doing what? He still couldn't wrap his brain around this conversation. Everything she said was a direct contradiction to his memory of that night. She'd cried as he'd driven her home, not huge hiccupping sobs but the silent kind. The kind that ripped at his gut. None of this made any sense.

Her head rose slowly, her eyes big and hopeful. "I'm not in love with you if that's what you're afraid of. I only want sex. Rough sex."

Evan nearly choked on his own spit. "Excuse me?"

"I'm sorry. I'm not explaining this very well. I'm just so nervous." She bit her lip. "Because if that's what's holding you back, you don't have to worry. I'm not looking for a relationship." Her ass scooted to the edge of the chair. "You see, since that night…" Teeth dug into her lower lip again. "God, this is embarrassing."

Sitting forward, he ran a hand over his face. "Believe me, nothing you can say will shock me." She'd already done that.

"The night we, um… I've never had that again."

"Sex?"

She laughed, reminding him of the long lazy days they'd shared by the lake. "I'm not dead. And I'm not frigid. I've had sex. And I usually have an orgasm. I just…it's never been so…"

He waited for her to come up with the words. Part of him was afraid to hear them. The other part already knew what they'd be and ached for the verbal confirmation.

"Freakin' hot!"

And there it was. Not that he wasn't glad he'd been wrong, but…

Evan rubbed both hands over his face. He needed to think and couldn't do that with her talking about hot sex and orgasms. His dick was coming back to life, but his head hurt with all the confusing information she'd thrown at him.

"Oh, god, I'm sorry." She jumped to her feet, a rosy flush spreading from her face to her chest and making her earlier blush pale in comparison. Feeling her way around the chair, she backed toward the door. "You're not into that."

"Shayna, I don't—"

"No, don't worry about it." She waved a hand and gave him a forced smile. "I get it."

Without another word, she disappeared, the pounding of her feet hitting the stairs competing with the blood pumping in his ears.

Going after her crossed his mind, but until he got his muddled brain clear, he probably wouldn't say or do anything that wouldn't make matters worse. Josh was right. He could see what others needed, how to fix them, but when it came to his own life, he was clueless. Or maybe it was just where Shayna was involved. She'd kept him off balance back then, and it was the same now.

Evan sank deep into the chair and closed his eyes. Flashes of that summer came rushing back. Her laughing as they swam in the cool water of the lake, her splashing him, then screaming when he gave chase. Pouting when he caught her and refused to let go. The flare of fiery passion in her eyes when she came apart in his arms.

That night, her eyes had been glazed over with alcohol-induced lust. He should have stopped her, but he'd been drunk himself. And the longer Evan watched Tucker's hands caress her bare skin as he fucked her mouth with his tongue, the more aroused Evan had become. The feelings were disturbing, and he tried to shove them aside. Yet the sensual undulation of her hips as she ground her pussy against another man had stirred his cock.

And it hadn't been enough.

Chapter Four

The wind picked up, coming off the lake to whip the flames of campfire into a frenzy. Much like the heat that streaked down Evan's spine straight to his cock as Shayna's lips surrounded the head of Tucker's dick. Evan went from turned-on to a full hard-on.

She tilted her head to one side, and her steamy gaze met his just before she dipped her head and took Tucker's erection deeper. Tucker groaned, and Evan swallowed his own, knowing how hot and wet and silky her mouth felt. Her cheeks hollowed, and this time he couldn't hold back the moan.

Withdrawing, she looked across the three feet between them and blinked a silent question.

"Don't stop," Tucker panted. He tried to pull her head closer.

Resisting his efforts, she began to pump his shaft and cast Evan another questioning glance. She must have seen the lust taking hold of him because her gaze lowered to his straining crotch. Those big brown eyes grew wide, and her hand faltered in rhythm. He hadn't realized he was stroking himself over his swimsuit.

A desire he'd never known drove him to lower his chin in assent.

With a deliberate slowness, she gathered her long hair to one side, giving him a clear view as she ran her tongue the length of Tucker's cock. Evan's breath hitched, and blood pounded up his shaft.

She continued to watch him as she sucked Tucker into her mouth and pumped harder. Fluid seeped from the slit of Evan's cockhead. Against his will, his hand reached inside his trunks and his fingers circled the girth. Watching him, she sucked harder, lips tight, cheeks indented, breasts heaving.

Fuck, she was hot. Incredibly hot. As into this…this…whatever the hell they were doing as he was.

"I'm coming." Tucker's hips jerked, and Shayna made a noise that shook Evan from the erotic haze. She didn't want to swallow.

Before he could move, she slapped Tucker's hands from her hair, slipped his wet dick from her mouth, and sat back on her heels. Using both hands, she milked him through release.

"Julie," Tucker muttered as jets of cum dribbled over her fingers.

Evan blew out a long breath, glad she hadn't swallowed, that Tucker wasn't thinking of her *as he came, and that he was a quick draw. And yet somewhere deep in the dark recesses of Evan's being, he hadn't wanted it to end.*

Shayna released Tucker's cock, sat back on her heals to stare at her hands, but didn't move otherwise. Nor did she speak as Tucker started to snore. She looked a little shaky.

"Tucker." Evan nudged Tucker with his foot.

The big lug roused enough to open his eyes. "Huh?"

Evan shoved him harder. "Go sleep it off in your truck."

Tucker grumbled but ambled to his feet, pulled his swimsuit up, and wove his way toward the truck parked on the other side of the fire.

"He won't remember any of this tomorrow." Even if he did, Evan would make sure he never mentioned it to a soul.

"Will you*?" Her voice was barely a whisper as she wiped her hands on the grass.*

How could he not? But he couldn't tell her he'd remember every detail as long as he lived.

But that wasn't true.

Oh, he had remembered some of it, most of it. His actions and the images of her hands and mouth on Tucker. But not her eyes, not the willingness, the excitement. He'd always put the blame for everything on his shoulders and his alone.

Evan rose abruptly from the chair, his heart pounding, fists clenched, dick hard—all the blatant lust from that night swirling inside him. Before tonight, when the memories of their last hours together seeped unwanted from the cracks and crevices of his twisted mind, he never remembered the brief minutes she'd been as aroused as he had.

He strode to the window and yanked the curtains back. The moon was out, full and bright against an inky backdrop. Fitting that the sky would mimic the one from his memories. The pale glow of its beams spilling over her porcelain skin. What else had he kept locked away?

Closing his eyes, he pressed his forehead against the windowpane, cool from the night air, and let the memories tumble free.

Every night before, when they'd reached this point, Evan felt as if a rope coiled around his chest, tightening with each labored gasp for air, with each touch of her slender fingers, each sweet lingering taste of her lips. But the cord had frayed over the summer, growing weaker. He wasn't sure what would happen if it broke so he'd held on to those threads for dear life.

And now they were unraveling at a rate he couldn't stop.

"I can't believe I just did that." Head down, she blinked several times and her throat worked nervously. "Are you mad?"

"No." He covered the distance between them, latched onto her upper arms, and hauled her against his chest. "I'm not mad."

She lifted her head, and the lingering hunger in her eyes would have knocked him to his knees if he hadn't already been on them. Her breath rushed in and out of her lungs, the warmth of each exhale bleeding through his shirt, searing his skin. Her breasts burned hotter, mashing against his ribs.

The proverbial rope snapped, and something broke loose inside him, something primal and raw. He had to taste her. His mouth covered hers, and he slashed his tongue between her swollen lips. Swollen from his long slow kisses and from stretching around Tucker's cock. Her mouth was hot, wet, and sweet as her tongue pursued his. The beast inside him demanded more.

With one hand, he gripped her hip and yanked her against his throbbing erection. He wound her hair into his other hand, fisting it tight to her scalp to angle her head as he plundered her mouth, teeth clashing, biting. A part of him wanted to punish her even though she hadn't done anything he didn't want her to do. He'd practically cheered her on.

A whimper drifted into his consciousness, but he ignored it. Her slender fingers tugged at his shirt, and he let go of her hip to capture her wrist to tuck it behind her back. She cried out, but he swallowed the sound and lowered her to the ground.

He'd wanted her since the first moment she smiled at him, and she'd begged him to fuck her every night as he brought her to pleasure with his mouth. Yet somehow, he'd managed to restrain himself. Tonight, though, a desperate need that reached far into his baser core drove him, as if he wouldn't breathe again unless he sank deep into her wet heat.

She bucked against him, and he pinned her with his weight. Letting go of her hand, he dragged one side of her bikini top down, felt it rip, and palmed her breast, squeezing the soft flesh. Her hips jolted beneath him again, and a moan hummed against his lips. He tore his mouth from hers and lowered his head to capture the taut nipple and a good portion surrounding it. He sucked hard, as hard as she'd sucked Tucker's dick.

Her fingers dove into his hair, holding him close, not pushing him away. "Evan."

The sound of her voice pulled at his senses, half warning him to listen and half urging him on. Whether Shayna pleaded for him to stop or to keep going, Evan didn't want to know, didn't want to stop. He abandoned her breast to stay her words with another punishing kiss and reached for the waistband of her shorts.

The button gave easily, the zipper a bit trickier. He gave up mid-way down and yanked the denim down to her knees. Her legs flailed, and the shorts went flying over their heads. The bottoms of her swimsuit tore away with hardly any effort. Her feminine scent wafted around him, filling his senses, heightening the red haze that drove him.

Her palm flattened against his chest as he angled to remove his shirt. He thrust her hand away and broke the kiss long enough to jerk the T-shirt over his head, but her hand returned to his waist. Again, he pushed it out of the way and worked his trunks down far enough that he could kick them off.

"Evan, please." Her breathy whisper hit him like an aphrodisiac.

Grasping her wrist as she reached for him again, he held it beside her head and shoved a knee between her thighs to spread them wide. With a twist of his lower body, he covered her slight frame with his heavier one, positioned his cock at her opening and moaned into her mouth. "I need you, Shay."

Her free hand caressed his face. "Yes."

Wet heat, his for the taking, kissed the crown of his cock. He didn't hesitate. One powerful thrust breached her slick passage. Her body stiffened beneath him, but he couldn't give her time to adjust. He had to move.

Drawing back, he slammed into her tight pussy. He repeated the action with a pounding force. His balls slapped against her ass, adding to the pleasure rippling up his spine. Thrust after thrust, he relished the velvety grip of her cunt. He'd known sex with Shayna would be good, but reality surpassed fantasy by a thousand percent.

His chest strove for more air, his dick for more depth. He untangled the hand from her hair, clasped the hollow behind her knee, and drew her leg to rest at his waist.

Shayna moaned and arched against him. Evan pumped faster, harder. He couldn't get deep enough. Couldn't breathe. He severed the kiss and sucked in a gulp of air. He raised her leg higher, outward. The next downward plunge seated him to the root.

"Fuck, yes." His balls constricted, and a tingle at the base of his back warned him he was about to come. "No."

A shrill cry pierced his eardrum just as her inner muscles squeezed his shaft like a tight fist. He let go of her hand and covered her mouth to muffle the sound, but he couldn't prevent the suction on his dick. Teeth locked onto his fingers and long nails scored his back, but the pain only added to the pleasure as hot cum shot through his shaft.

Thrusting deep, he stilled and rode the powerful wave that dragged him under, drowning him in the darkest, sweetest ecstasy. He didn't fight it, didn't want to be rescued.

Then a soft sniffling sound pulled at him, trying to penetrate through the darkness. This he did fight. Another wet sniff that wouldn't be ignored yanked him from the black waters. He opened his eyes, and the heart that had beat furiously moments ago stalled as a tear spilled from the corner of Shayna's eye and rolled into the hair at her temple.

Throat constricting, Evan clutched the curtains on either side of the window. He couldn't breathe for the guilt he'd felt in that moment when he realized Shayna was crying.

But now he'd allowed himself to remember more clearly *her* actions as well as his. She hadn't been fighting him. Her tongue had been eager for his. Her pleas weren't for him to stop. She'd tried to help him undress, not push him away. And she'd found just as much pleasure from their violent coupling as he had. She'd even said she loved him when he dropped her off that night.

Yet her tears had made him second-guess himself and he'd lived with the belief that he'd hurt her in the worst way a man could hurt a woman.

And he'd been afraid to say the words, to make it real. Sorry wouldn't have begun to repair what he thought he'd done. But his fear and guilt had kept him from knowing the truth. One word would have spared them both the heartache his leaving had caused. He hadn't understood how she could forgive him.

According to Shayna, she'd never felt there was anything to forgive and eagerly asked for the pain he'd inflicted. For a mere moment, his body welcomed the idea. The restless beast roared with hunger as images of the things he could do to her ran through his mind, whetting its enormous appetite.

Opening his eyes, Evan inhaled a calming breath and slowly released it. Not could do. *Would* do. Things he *would* do to her. But first, they had to talk. Just because she said she liked her sex a little on the rough side didn't mean she would enjoy what he was willing to offer. He wasn't the boy she remembered, once out of control and dangerous. He was a Dom who liked his submissive bound and vulnerable to his whim, whether that included a bit of pain to foster the pleasure or not.

But if she heard him out and still wanted to

play, then maybe he'd finally exorcise a ghost.

He turned from the window and strode from the room toward the stairs. Fuck, he was hard, but it was too late to talk tonight, and dust coated his hide an inch thick. A cold shower would remedy both. Jacking off would feel better, but he much preferred controlling his needs. Now that his need focused on Shayna, restraint was even more important.

The cold water of the shower not only washed away the filth of a hard day's work and softened his cock, it also helped clear his head. By the time he towel-dried his hair in front of the mirror, his left brain had taken over. He had his opening argument planned. He'd brief her with the facts of the BDSM lifestyle he lived so that she could make an informed decision of whether to pursue this…whatever it was.

He wrapped the towel around his hip and brushed his teeth. As he placed the toothbrush in the cup by the sink, his knuckles bumped Shayna's electric toothbrush and knocked over the handset. Setting it back on the charger, he smiled at how she'd looked with toothpaste on her lips. Not exactly how he'd pictured her behind the door but cute and sexy all the same.

Opening the bathroom door, he made sure the hall was clear since he'd forgotten to grab clean clothes beforehand, then turned off the light and headed down the hall. Shayna was probably fast asleep, but that didn't stop him from slowing as he neared her room. The mere thought of her lying on the bed made him want to open the door, just for one look.

He reached for the knob but froze halfway there as a breathy moan sifted under the door. In contrast to the delicate sound, a more severe drone persisted with a steady two-beat rhythm, one slightly stronger than the other. *Buzz-buzz. Buzz-buzz.*

Evan glanced back the way he'd come at the bathroom door. Unless she had more than one electric toothbrush…

****

A fourth micro-orgasm waned, leaving Shayna breathless, sweaty, and wholly unsatisfied. She dragged the capsule-shaped vibrator to the other side of her clit, searching for another patch of sensitive nerves. Horny didn't begin to describe the ache in her core.

After throwing herself at Evan and having him reject her—again—she would have thought herself cured of any need of sex for a lifetime much less the time it would take to fall asleep. She hadn't lasted ten minutes before the fantasies had begun and the sheets caressed her skin into a fever. Shedding the linen hadn't helped. Not as images of Evan in the shower toyed with her libido.

Rejected or not, she still wanted him. And hearing the water run, she'd imagined his strong hands lathering the soap over his hard, bronzed torso. Up and over his pecs, down those ripped abs, around the steely length of his cock.

Her pussy clamped around wishful thinking, and she mourned its emptiness. Damn, if only she'd packed her dildo.

A creak at the foot of the bed penetrated the sexual hum in her ears. She fumbled for the main unit that controlled the speed of the vibrator, clicked it off, and listened.

"Finish." The deep, rich rasp boomed in the dimly lit room.

Eyes flying open, Shayna lurched upright, drawing her knees together and toward her body to cover her nakedness and the fact that she held a vibrator between her legs. "Evan?"

He bent toward her, grabbed her ankles, then slowly unfolded and spread them wide. "Finish."

A hot flush of arousal oozed through her body. "How long have you been standing there?"

"Long enough." He released the towel from his waist and let it drop to the floor. His stiff erection arrowed high, reaching for his bellybutton. Ropey veins threaded down the shaft, and his pearly essence glistened at the crown.

Lifting her gaze to his face, she tried to make out his expression, but it was cast in shadows. "I thought—"

"Finish it, Shayna." He gripped his cock in a tight fist and stroked from base to tip, thumbing the slick slit. "Now."

She swallowed the sudden rush of saliva and decided not to question his change of heart. Not yet anyway. He seemed intent on watching her masturbate, and if that led to what she hoped it would, she'd do anything he asked.

Slowly, she lay back down and pressed the button on the vibrator until she found the favored setting, then touched the buzzing oval to the top of her clit. She hissed in a breath, and her hips jerked as a delicious streak of icy heat shot down her thighs and curled her toes.

"I swear, Shayna, you push me to the end of my rope." He pumped a slow rhythm up and down his shaft.

God, that was hot. She'd never watched a man masturbate before. It made her want to make him enjoy watching her even more. She slid her free hand over her hip and toward the rise of her belly, then up along her ribcage and under the mound of her breast. Her beaded nipple tightened as her thumb grazed the flesh around the areola. A shiver skated over her skin, and she bit her lip, eyes scrunched tight, to keep from moaning.

With her thumb and forefinger, she pinched the nipple and rolled it as she once again pressed the vibrator to her swollen nub. A fifth mini-gasm shimmied through her. Her heels dug into the mattress. Her hips locked, and her pussy convulsed for a few brief seconds but found no gratification.

Rough hands took the frustrating toy from her hand. "My turn."

Shayna opened her eyes, eager to see him *finish* himself off.

Instead, he placed one knee on the bed, then hesitated. "Condom?"

Her heart beat faster as she rolled to the side of the bed and tore open the drawer. The box she'd bought on her way out of Austin ripped under her trembling fingers, and a strip of condoms spilled onto the sheet. A hand closed around her ankle, and she barely had time to snatch one up before he hauled her back to the middle of the bed.

A thrill she hadn't felt in nine years sucked the breath from her lungs. This was it, what she'd longed for. He took the packet from her, and she hated the time it took to open the resistant plastic. She needed his hands on her, firm and unrelenting, fingers digging, punishing. "Please hurry."

The latex rolled down his thick shaft, and she spread her legs wide. He crawled up her body, and her belly fluttered. She reached for him, but his fingers wrapped around her wrists, biting into her flesh and shoving her hands above her head.

"You want rough sex, Shayna?" His breath warmed her cheek as he settled on his knees between her legs.

She bucked her hips so that the head of his cock brushed her clit. "Yes, Evan, fuck me hard."

"I'll give you what you need." He took both her hands in one of his and palmed her hip with the other, pressing her into the mattress. "But we'll do this my way."

Shayna was trapped beneath his strong hands, helpless, unable to move except for her legs. And she loved every second of it. If only he'd—

The broad crown nudged her opening, then pushed forward into her greedy cunt. The slow inch-by-inch penetration was like feeding whiskey to an alcoholic one drop at a time. It was almost painful, which made it oh so delightful.

"You feel good, Shay."

His words nearly yanked her from the euphoric bliss, reminding her of the times she'd taken him into her mouth. She'd longed to hear them again, wished more than once over the years that he'd said them that night. He hadn't. But he said them now and somehow that made up for it. "Not as good as you."

The walls of her pussy stretched to make room for his engorged cock, then closed in around him, squeezing tight enough that she felt the pulse of his blood through the latex. The ridge around the head grazed her G-spot, and sweet ecstasy rippled through her.

She tried to move, needing him to repeat the action, but his fingers dug into her hip, the pain driving her pleasure higher. "Oh, god, yes."

A grunt, followed by more pressure, accompanied his withdrawal, and she wasn't sure if she wanted to lament the loss of his cock or rejoice in the added pain. The driving force of his thrust resolved the dilemma. Jagged shards of pleasure wrenched a cry from her throat.

Shifting his hips, he pulled out again. "Wrap your legs around my waist."

Without a moment's hesitation, she complied and promptly dug her heels into his ass, urging him to move. He chuckled but didn't disappoint as he slammed into her, deeper this time.

The edges of the pleasure-pain grew sharper, but it wasn't enough. "Move, Evan. Faster."

"I'm going to let go of your hands, but keep them where they are. Do you hear me, Shayna?"

"Yes, but I need you to move." She contracted her inner muscles around him, trying to convey her desperation.

"My way, remember?" He let go of her wrists, curled his fingers into her hair, and tilted her head back until she looked up at his face. His jaw clenched, and the vein in his forehead bulged. He obviously struggled for control. She lifted a hand to brush the golden hair from his eyes, but he reared his head back. "I said not to move your hands. If you can't follow my instructions, we'll stop right now. Do you understand?"

She let her arm drop, frustrated and confused by his rigid demand, but with a nod, she locked her hands together above her head. "Fine."

"Good." His grip in her hair tightened, and the sting seeped down her neck and into her shoulders. Then he flexed his hips. A long slow backward glide, then the powerful spearing plunge that would have shoved her toward the headboard had he not been holding her down.

A cry slipped past her lips as a shudder of bliss shook her from head to toe. She arched for more, but the heel of his hand ground her farther into the bed. Again, that helpless feeling, along with the rocking of his pubic bone against her clit, notched her lust higher.

Over and over, he repeated the gentle yet brutal pattern, keeping on her on the brink of orgasm but refusing to let her fly. Air resisted the draw of her lungs. Moisture beaded her brow and slipped into her hair. Her muscles burned. And through it all, Evan's gaze remained glued to her face, never wavering.

Shayna found the intensity almost too

overwhelming. She closed her eyes, shutting out everything but the sensations he evoked, afraid of the emotions that welled inside her. For the first time in nine years, she experienced the beauty of erotic bliss she'd ached for.

A sob ripped from her throat, and tears threatened to spill. "Please."

She wasn't sure he heard her until his lips feathered hers for a brief moment before he initiated a relentless pounding tempo.

"Come for me, Shay."

The deep coaxing command, gentle yet demanding, hurled her over the edge. The bite of his fingers, the prickle of her scalp, the hard punishing thrust of his cock—it was all too much. Wave after wave of heavenly pleasure washed over her, and she drifted along, content to stay right where she was forever.

"Fuck." He drove harder, faster, shallower. He surged deep and groaned. The pulsing heat of his cum filled the condom as he joined her.

Gradually, the euphoria lifted and his hold on her body eased. Another kiss brushed her forehead, her cheek, her lips. She opened her eyes as he eased his semi-erect cock from her still-spasming pussy.

He gently lifted her, repositioned her higher on the bed, pulled the sheet over her, and sat up. "Are you okay?"

A lump of emotion she was afraid to analyze lodged in her throat, so she nodded.

"You sure?" The back of his knuckles brushed across her cheek. "You're crying."

Shayna laughed and choked on a sob at the same time as she pushed herself up against the headboard, sheet clutched to her chest.

"I'm sorry." She finger-combed her hair off her face with one hand, then scrubbed the tears away as they fell. "I don't usually react like this. It was just so..."

"Freakin' hot?" He teased her with that panty-stealing smile.

Another laugh bubbled forth, and she nodded again. "This was what I've been looking for all these years, but nothing I tried ever worked. It was never the same as when...well, you know."

He smiled again, but even in the dimly lit room, she could tell it never reached his eyes. "We'll talk in the morning."

"You're not staying?"

"You should get some sleep."

"And I won't sleep if you stay?"

"No." He leaned forward to kiss her lightly on the cheek, then backed away. "No, you won't."

He stood and walked around the bed, bending to swipe the towel off the floor as he padded on bare feet to the door.

He was leaving, and she still didn't know if this was all there'd be. "Evan?"

He swung the door open and paused, his body a dark silhouette.

How was she supposed to ask him if there would be more? "Is this it?"

"Do you want this to be it?"

"No." *Hell no.* She wanted more. Right now. All night. All tomorrow. A whole week of Evan wouldn't be enough to make up for the last nine years. It sure as hell wouldn't be enough to make up for the years ahead without him.

"Then, no, this is not it. Not by a long shot."

Chapter Five

"You're a happy camper this morning."

Shayna stopped humming and smiled at Josh over her shoulder as he crutch-hopped into the kitchen. "I slept really great last night."

Really, really great. She hadn't slept that good in years. No tossing and turning, just dead to the world sleep. And she'd woken up eager to greet the day and whatever it brought. Especially if it was more sex with Evan.

Turning the bacon over, she began to hum again.

"Hmm, you sure it didn't have anything to do with the bump and grind going on upstairs?"

Her heart lurched and her face flamed as she swung to face him. "You heard?"

A grin pulled at his lips. "No, darlin'. But your face says it all."

"Oh, my god." She turned away and stared at the grease popping in the skillet. Was she that transparent?

His low chuckle filled the room.

The heat in her cheeks grew hotter. "You're an

ass sometimes. Did you know that?"

"Oh, come on, darlin'." He sat in the chair behind her and pulled her onto his good leg.

She swatted at him with the tongs. "Don't darlin' me."

He caught her wrist before she could smack him. "Hey, I'm happy for you and Ev. At least someone around here is getting laid."

"Something smells good." Evan's decadent voice and the scuff of his boots on the wood floor in the hall sent Shayna into a panic.

Josh let her go, and she jumped off his lap as Evan entered the kitchen. She hurried to the refrigerator, hoping to cool the redness of her cheeks. "Hungry?"

When he didn't answer, she straightened and twisted to look at him. He stood just inside the door, his gaze narrowed on Josh as he hid behind a newspaper. Evan turned his attention on her, and damn it, she blushed to her roots again.

In three strides, he crossed the room, pulled her out of the refrigerator, slammed the door, and flattened her against the cold, metal wall with his hard body. His mouth covered hers, his tongue demanding entrance. She didn't deny him but savored the taste of him, all mint and man, as his tongue explored the roof of her mouth, the hollow of her cheek, and under her tongue.

A strong hand cupped the back of her head,

angling her to deepen the kiss. His other hand rested on her hip, squeezing into the bruises he'd left the night before. She moaned and arched into his grip. He thrust a thigh between her legs and ground into her. He was hard beneath the denim, which made her moan again. Moisture gathered at the mouth of her pussy. If he fucked her right here, against the refrigerator, she wouldn't argue.

Then his tongue slowed, and the pressure against her body eased. He nipped at her lips with his teeth.

"I'm going out to fix the fence by the lake." His voice was low and hushed, reminding her that Josh sat only a few feet away.

Out of breath, she nodded. "Okay."

The hand at her nape slid to palm her cheek, and his eyes followed the path of his thumb over her bottom lip. "There's a black bag in the back seat of my truck. Go look through it."

"Why?"

He lifted his hungry gaze to meet hers. "After you see what's inside, you might not want this to continue. I'll understand if you don't." He lowered his forehead to hers. "But if you do, bring the bag out to the lake around noon."

"Okay."

Evan stepped back and sauntered to the back door. He grabbed his hat and settled it over his blond head. Not for the first time, her gaze lingered on the way his hair curled upward in the back, reaching for the brim. And how the sides fell over the tips of his ears. Her fingers itched to touch the softness.

"Shay?"

Her attention snapped back to his face. "Yeah?"

"Keys are on my dresser." He opened the back door and paused. "And Shay?"

She lifted a brow for further instructions. The man was getting bossy. She kind of liked it.

"I'll be hungry."

The wolfish glint in his eyes left no doubt that he didn't mean for food. Her peaked nipples tingled as he walked out the door. She meandered to the screen door to soak in the sight of him until he disappeared into the barn.

God, the man could kiss. She lifted her fingers to her lips. She'd forgotten how talented his mouth was. He'd barely kissed her night before last when she'd laid one on him. And the barely there kisses last night didn't qualify.

"Shayna?"

She sighed at Josh's intrusion. She wanted to follow Evan, to drag him into a stall, and pick up where they'd left off. "Huh?"

"Bacon's burning."

"Oh, shit." She spun around and ran to the

stove. The bacon was black, and the vent couldn't suck up the smoke fast enough. Snatching up a hot pad from the counter, she shoved the skillet to another burner and flipped off the gas. "Shit, shit, shit."

"That's okay." Josh folded his newspaper and grinned. "Even if I had breakfast, I'd still be *hungry* all day after the show you two put on."

Too irritated to be embarrassed by his innuendo, Shayna leaned back against the sink and folded her arms over her chest. "What's your problem this morning?"

"I don't have a problem that a little alone time and some hand cream won't fix." He pushed back from the table and stood next to the counter. The bulge in his pants managed to draw the heat to her face again as he reached for a box of cereal.

She couldn't help remembering how Evan had stood at the foot of her bed and stroked himself. Imagining Josh doing the same thing did funny things to her insides.

"That was for my benefit, ya know." Josh sat back down, opened the box, and stuffed a handful of dry cereal into his mouth.

Glad he'd changed the subject, she plopped into a chair beside him and stuck her hand in the box for her own handful. "What are you talking about?"

"That show. Ev was staking his claim. To

make sure I know who you belong to."

The idea of belonging to Evan sent tiny, winged creatures flying in her tummy. She stomped them down. It was just sex. Really great, no strings attached, freakin' hot sex. After Josh's casts came off, Evan would return to Houston and she'd be back in Austin. "I don't belong to anyone."

"While you're here, you do. Last night sealed the deal. He was letting me know I can look all I want but no touching." He laughed. "Course, I had to give him a little shove this morning to get him to claim you."

Shayna stared at him with her mouth open. "You did that on purpose, didn't you? You knew he was about to walk in when you—"

"Heard his boots on the stairs." He shrugged. "Just doin' what I can to help."

She punched his arm. "You are so bad."

"Ha! You know you enjoyed the results. I sure did."

Had she enjoyed being squashed against the refrigerator with Evan's tongue fucking her mouth and his hand branding her ass? Hell, yeah. Enjoyed being labeled property? The independent part of her said no, but the soft feminine part of her said yes. She liked Evan's possessive behavior. Especially when it led to yummy kisses. And she liked feeling possessed, as if she were his to cherish, to take care of.

"So now that we've had breakfast"—he rolled up the cereal sack and closed the box—"I guess you'll be off to look in that bag."

"Maybe." She stuffed her mouth full of little round o's to keep from admitting her curiosity was piqued.

"I've seen what's in that bag, and I can tell you, my brother's into some kinky shit."

Kinky? As in rough sex kinky? Blindfolds? Handcuffs? She could get into that. Just the thought of Evan handcuffing her made her wet. "What do you mean?"

"You'll see." He took her hand in his and squeezed. "All I'm saying is, when you make your decision, be very certain it's what you want."

She frowned and tugged her hand free. "You're making me nervous."

"Good. You need to be. Don't do this just to make him happy either." He stood heavily on his good leg and put the box on the counter, then circled back around. "'Cause if you're not honest, he'll know, and you'll lose him."

"I don't have him to begin with." Didn't want him beyond their time here. It was just sex.

"Whatever you say." With that, Josh left the kitchen.

She followed him down the hall. "Do you

need anything?"

"Nope. I'm good for a while." He turned into the den, and she took the stairs.

In Evan's bedroom, she found the keys on the dresser, right where he said they'd be. The room was clean, neat, void of clutter or knick-knacks except for the bull riding trophies on a shelf. The bed was made. His house in Houston was probably as sparse. She imagined the furnishings, all black with chrome and glass. White carpet.

She wandered to the closet and smiled. Definitely OCD. His clothes hung according to the garment. Shirts from dark to light. Dress pants then jeans, again from dark to light. His shoes and boots lined the back wall, laces tied. He loved order. Probably why he'd become a lawyer.

So where did the kink come in?

"Guess I'll find out."

Excitement forced her feet out the door, down the stairs, and through the back door to where the family parked behind the house. His truck was next to her car. A four-door monster. Most folks said men with big trucks were compensating for something, but Evan had no shortcomings. At least not physically.

He'd said the bag was in the back, so she unlocked the back passenger door with the key fob and climbed up. The interior was as clean as his room but hot as freakin' hell. She climbed over the console, jammed her foot on the brake, and punched the button in the ignition. She cranked up the air and slid back to the rear.

Settling onto the gray leather seat, she unzipped the big black bag, pulled back the top flap, and blinked. Holy freakin' shit.

****

Sweat poured off Evan as he tightened the barbed wire on the last post. Noon had come and gone a half hour ago. Shayna wasn't coming.

Dammit to hell. He chucked the wire stretcher in the toolbox with a force that closed the lid. Maybe the black bag was too much. He should have waited, introduced her to his needs more slowly.

But she'd responded to him last night with the fervor of an experienced, if not seasoned, sub. She liked the dominance, handing over her body and her will so eagerly. She'd relished the pain.

And afterward, she'd been a mess—a hot, sexy as hell mess. Hair tangled, black smudges of mascara on her pale cheeks from swiping at her tears, dark eyes pleading with him. She'd wanted him to stay. And fuck, he'd wanted to.

For the first time since he'd become a Dom, he wanted to break his own rules. He wanted to slide under the sheet and soak in the comfort of her soft, warm body. To feel the rise and fall of her breast under his hand as she drifted into slumber.

To smell the vanilla shampoo in her hair as he followed.

The need was strong, and it had taken every ounce of his control to walk out of her room. He didn't share a bed with a woman longer than it took to fuck her. Sharing a bed meant intimacy, and he couldn't afford that kind of intimacy, especially not with Shayna.

And now he was glad he'd held firm.

Getting further involved with her would only turn out badly. Last night had awakened more than his memories. Feelings he hadn't acknowledged in nine years kept pushing their way to the surface. Not good. It had taken too long to get over her before. He wasn't sure he could do it again.

Not that he regretted having sex with her. If anything, it had calmed the beast raging inside him. Taking control, letting his Dom out… God, that had felt good. He definitely had to find a new partner.

Wiping a sleeve across his brow, he squinted against the sun at the dust billowing on the other side of the rise. He hefted the toolbox and trekked a few feet to Josh's old, beat-up ranch truck. As he stowed the tools in the back, his pickup crested the hill.

That doesn't mean it's her or that she's here for you. She was probably here to tell him face-to-face what a sick fuck he was.

He hopped up to sit on the tailgate, removed his gloves, and waited.

The truck pulled up close, but the dark tint of the windows hid the driver until the glass rolled down. She smiled, a bit unsure. "Sorry, I'm late. You still hungry?"

Every ounce of tension unfurled. Every doubt that he shouldn't move forward with his plan to introduce Shayna to BDSM vanished. In their place, the blazing coil of arousal tightened. "Starving."

Her cheeks tinted pink, and she lowered her gaze to his boots. "Should I just wait for you to finish?"

"All done." He dropped to his feet, crossed the few yards between them, and leaned against the door of his truck. "Why don't you go on down and wait for me? I want to take a swim to wash off and cool down."

Dark sooty lashes lifted, and her soft, brown eyes stared up at him. Excitement and a hint of fear radiated from their depths—both a good sign. Her hair was pulled back in a ponytail. It would have to come down. But for now, it served a purpose.

Reaching through the window, he captured the thick tail and used it to lure her closer. He ducked his head and slid his mouth over her parted lips. His tongue dipped inside for a languid exploration. She tasted sweet, like strawberries, and smelled just as good. Fresh, flowery, innocent. A little sound escaped her throat, and blood streamed to his cock.

Yep, he definitely needed some cooling down.

Evan lightened the kiss to a slow meeting of the lips, then drew back and released her hair. "I'll only be a few minutes."

She nodded as he stepped away. Shifting into drive, she turned the truck around and drove toward the lake. His body hummed, tense with the need to dominate, the coil of rope around his chest drawing tight.

Last night might have taken the edge off, but it only whetted his appetite for more.

****

Knees tucked to her chest, Shayna sat on a quilt under the willow. It had grown over the years, weeping farther over the bank and dipping its branches into the water. The pier, about a hundred feet away, had aged as well, the planks gray and warped. Minutes ago, she'd watched Evan dive off the end, buck naked. He swam a ways out, then swam back and hauled himself out of the water.

Her skin heated even in the shade as he stood with his back to her in the bright sunlight, his tall frame wet and glistening, golden brown with grooves etched in all the right places. Broad shoulders, trim waist, long legs…perfection.

Covering that body was a crime, but cover it he did as he dragged on his jeans, not bothering with the boxer-briefs he'd removed. He gathered his boots and shirt and sauntered along the pier and up the hill. He bent to avoid the lower branches and laid his clothes near the blanket. Water still ran in small rivulets over his bare chest.

She sighed inwardly. One had to be content with small favors.

"Hey." He plopped onto the quilt, eating up all the space with his large body and even larger presence and setting her nerves into overdrive.

"I brought you some lunch." Rising to her knees, she started pulling food from the cooler next to her. She handed him a sandwich. "Want something to drink? I brought beer."

"Got anything else?"

She gave him a teasing grin. "And here I thought you'd want a cold one after a hard half day's work."

"Normally I would. But I like to keep a clear head during a session."

A bottle of water slipped from her trembling fingers, splashing into the melting ice. "Session?"

"That *is* why we're here, Shay."

Heat blooming in her cheeks, she snagged the

bottle by the lid and held it out.

Instead of taking it from her, he clasped her wrist. "If you're not here for that, you shouldn't have come. If you've changed your mind, you need to go now."

Shayna slowly sat back down and faced him with as much confidence as she could muster. "I'm here because I want… I just didn't know you called it that."

He released her, accepted the water, and took a bite of the sandwich. "You gonna eat?"

She was nervous enough. Eating in front of Evan, knowing what would happen when they were done… She could barely swallow. No way in hell would she have kept anything down. "I ate with Josh."

A frown puckered his golden brows. "Is there something going on between you two?"

The question didn't surprise her after Josh's stunt that morning, but his reasoning did. "Because I ate lunch with him?"

"You seem pretty comfortable together."

Anger bubbled up inside her. "Do you think I'd be out here if I was fucking Josh?"

"I didn't ask if you were fucking him. But there's more to your relationship than either of you is saying."

"We became close after you left. Not close like

you think, though I won't say it didn't cross my mind or hasn't since. He was there. You weren't. I had needs. But we never went there. We were friends."

He snorted. "I know my brother. He'd take whatever you offered."

"I don't think you know him at all." And she'd leave it at that. Evan didn't have the right to know about the kiss or that Josh had been the one to say no. "He's just pushing buttons, yours and mine." She looked out over the water, afraid to see his reaction to her next statement. "He thinks we're going to get back together."

Except for the buzz of cicadas, silence reigned under the thick canopy. Obviously, he believed otherwise, as she did, which shouldn't have hurt. But maybe Josh was right. Maybe she did harbor a small hope, a very small hope, that Evan still held some kind of affection for her.

A glutton for punishment, outside the bedroom as well as in, she turned her head to look at him. "Can I ask you a question?"

"Sure."

"Did you know I'd be here? When you agreed to come help Josh?"

"No, my brother didn't disclose that bit of information." He polished off the last of his sandwich and swigged down half the bottle of water.

"If you'd known, would you have come?" *You just can't get enough.*

"I don't know, Shay. Probably not."

Tears burned the back of her eyes. She turned away, blinking to dry the moisture.

"But not because of you," he went on. "I'm the one with a problem."

She looked at him again. His blue eyes were intense, haunted. "But your problem is with me, isn't it?"

"It was."

"Was?"

"I hurt you, or at least I thought I had. I was so out of control I don't know if I'd have been able to stop if you said no."

"Evan, I was as out of control as you. And I didn't want you to stop."

"I realize that now." He shook his head, and the haunted look in his eyes turned tortured. "But god, that night I scared the shit out of myself. Subconsciously, I knew you were into it, at least I hope I knew." He blew out a breath. "I don't know. I was blind to anything but my own driving needs. And then after, you kept crying and in my mind that meant you weren't into it or that I'd hurt you somehow. I didn't know what to do."

Of all the reasons he'd have left her, this was never one she considered. "That's why you left?"

"Yes."

"What? You thought I'd cry rape?"

"No, I never considered that." He rubbed the back of his neck. "You probably could have."

"Evan, I was as much to blame for what happened as you." *And I loved you.* "If you'd have bothered to talk to me, I'd have told you as much."

"I know." He inhaled deeply and blew out a breath. "I don't expect you to understand, but I didn't leave because I was afraid of what I'd done. Well, not for that reason alone. I was afraid I'd do it again. I liked it, Shayna. I liked holding you down. I liked knowing the pressure of my fingers would leave bruises on your beautiful body. And god, the noises you made, those were sounds of pain, and they triggered a need to hear them again."

His words should have scared her, too. Instead, the picture he painted in her mind made her breasts feel heavy. Tiny threads of pleasure streaked from the nipple to her core. If she'd worn panties, they'd have been wet. "I liked it, too."

"But Shayna, I didn't want to like it. I didn't like losing control like that. I tried to block out everything that happened. I tried to forget, but I couldn't."

Just me. You forgot me.

He sighed. "It took me a long time to figure

out it was okay to want those things."

"Which is how you got into whatever it is that requires the contents of your black bag?" She waved a hand toward his truck. The bag would have made her more nervous than she already was, so she'd left it out of sight.

"Yes."

She rested her chin on her knees and stared ahead. If only he'd talked to her, they could have worked it all out. She'd have been willing to experiment. They might have still been together. No, that was a dangerous presumption. But she could lay one of his concerns to rest. "I cried that night because of the overwhelming power of that orgasm. Not because I was hurt or ashamed or any other reason. Just the magnitude of that one incredible moment and everything that led to it."

And because I loved you so much it hurt.

Again silence filled the space between them. She wasn't sure what to say or if anything she said would convince him she wanted to move beyond the past and get down to a little black bag business.

"Shay?"

"Hmm?"

"We don't have to do this."

She tilted her head to the side and frowned. "I'm beginning to think you don't want to."

"I just need you to be sure."

Shayna sighed. "I don't know how else to convince you I'm sure."

Maybe words weren't needed. Maybe she needed to show him. Rising to her feet, she slipped off her sandals and tossed them in the grass behind her. She grabbed the hem of her dress, pulled it over her head, and laid it over the cooler. Standing before him in nothing but a toe ring, she let her arms relax at her sides.

His gaze raked over her body, pausing at her freshly groomed pussy that probably glistened with her juices, then again at her breasts. Finally, his gaze locked with hers. "I'd say that's pretty convincing."

Chapter Six

Evan slung the black duffel over his shoulder and shut the door of his truck. The proverbial rope around his chest tightened as he made his way back to the willow. Having Shayna talk about what she wanted and then strip naked had stirred the Dom in him.

The need to possess her, to control her pleasure, to provide or withhold it… He almost couldn't breathe the urge to begin was so great. Yet half the pleasure was not giving in to that urge too soon but letting the need build. The other half would be prolonging hers, hearing her plead for release, and then deciding when to allow it.

He dropped the bag beside the blanket, ready for the slow and exquisite torture of verbal foreplay. "Before we begin, there are a few more things we need to discuss."

"Oh." She blinked a few times and turned to pick up her dress.

"No." His sharp tone made her jump, just as he intended. "I want to look at you while we talk."

She slowly straightened, brows furrowing deep in confusion. "You want me to stand here naked while we talk?"

"Yes."

Her dark eyes flashed with heat, and he wasn't sure if she was excited by the idea of baring herself to him in broad daylight or by his command. He intended to find out.

"Okay." Arms at her sides, she rolled her shoulders back, lifting her full breasts, nipples taut, pink, and beckoning him to taste her. "So, what do you want to talk about?"

Evan tore his gaze from her long, slender body to watch her face carefully. "First, did you look in the bag like I told you? You know what's in here?"

Sooty lashes fluttered as her lids lowered to conceal her thoughts from him, but her cheeks flushed a bright shade of pink that spread to her breasts. "Yes."

"Then you know what's in store for you if we continue?"

"I have a general idea."

"And you're willing?"

Her eyelids lifted, revealing the slight dilation of her pupils. Her gaze was steady as it held his. "Yes, I'm willing to let you do whatever you want."

Satisfied she wasn't leaping into this totally blind, he squatted next to the bag and unzipped the closure. "You mentioned last night that you've tried to find what you need. Rough sex."

"Yeah?" Her voice sounded wary but curious.

Letting her stew in her curiosity, he pulled back the flap. A ball gag lay on top, and the thought of using it on Shayna tempted him. To see her lips stretched around the sphere like he'd seen them stretched around Tucker's—

No, today was all about learning on both their parts, and they couldn't do that if she couldn't communicate. Besides, he wanted to hear her scream when he made her come.

He moved the gag to the side, pulled out a length of black nylon rope, tucked it in the back of his jeans, and reached for a set of black leather wrist cuffs.

Rising, he motioned for her hands. She obeyed without question, holding out her wrists with an eagerness that pleased him. As the cuffs fastened around the delicate white flesh, the tightness in his chest eased and his cock stretched to fill his jeans. With that one simple task, he slipped deeper into the dark, primal place that housed the hungry beast.

Clipping the metal chain that was attached to one cuff to the ring on the other bound her hands with only five inches of space between them. "Feel okay?"

She tested the constraints. "Mmmhmm."

He took the rope from the back waist of his jeans and began to unravel it. "Tell me how you tried to find it."

"What do you mean?"

"Rough sex. Did you ask someone? A boyfriend? A lover?"

"Oh." She nodded then shook her head. "The first time, yes. The guy I was seeing at the time. He might have become a boyfriend if I hadn't told him I wanted him to get rough with me."

He looped the rope around the chain between the cuffs and began a square knot. "What happened?"

She lifted a shoulder and let it drop. "His idea of rough was quick on, quick off. I never even got started."

"You said the first time. What else happened?"

A huge sigh forewarned the frustration with what came next. "Two in a row left without making it to third base. They thought I was nuts. The last time…"

A tremor shook her body as he finished the knot. He glanced up to find her bottom lip clenched tight between her teeth. Her gaze darted everywhere but at him. Whatever she didn't want to say couldn't be good.

Using a finger to tip her chin, he forced her to make eye contact. "Tell me."

"Long story short, I met a guy at a bar. I told him what I was looking for. He didn't look at me like I was crazy, so I asked him home with me. I don't normally do that, but I was desperate. Things were going as I'd hoped, but then…his hands were…" Her hands flitted to her throat. "I couldn't breathe."

Son of a bitch. He dropped his hand and stepped back, as if his own hands barred the air from her lungs. His stomach rolled. She could have been seriously injured—or killed. Even the most skilled Doms didn't venture into breath play without training. He'd never been interested in learning.

She rubbed the base of her throat. "I'm just glad he finished before I lost consciousness. That was three years ago, and needless to say, I've stuck with boring sex ever since."

"You don't have to settle, Shay."

She smiled and indicated her imprisoned hands. "Now that you're here, I don't."

If she could talk about it and still want to move forward with their session, she was made of stronger stuff than he'd given her credit for. But she'd had time to get over the near tragedy while anger raged through him at the man who hurt her. And at the same time, a familiar guilt threatened to overwhelm him.

But her teasing smile squashed that demon

and reminded him the reason for his guilt didn't exist anymore.

"I'm just saying you have to be more careful." Shaking off the morose thoughts, he tossed the rope over the tree limb above their heads, then lobbed it over the branch next to it for leverage. "There are places to find what you're looking for."

"What kind of places?"

"Fetish clubs or dungeons where members are vetted and trained in all aspects of BDSM." With a tug, he watched as her hands were slowly drawn above her head. The rope grew taut, her arms extended high.

"BDSM? Isn't that like whips, chains, black leather, and flogging?"

"It can be. But it's about much more than that." He pulled again, a little harder.

She gasped, and her full breasts bounced as her heels left the ground. Another inch and she balanced on tiptoes.

He tied off the rope and turned to admire his handy work.

Beautiful. The sleek length of her body stretched like a ballerina. Her pale skin was flawless, dappled shadows from the leaves overhead dancing across its perfection. Black lashes fanned her cheeks then lifted, revealing the expressive brown eyes that had haunted him. Now, though, they were clear of fear and full of trust.

In fact, she didn't seem at all fazed to be dangling from the end of his rope. Other than the catch in her breathing, she could have been talking to him over the breakfast table. She had no idea what was in store for her.

The residue of anger he'd felt toward the man who hurt her ignited. Her lack of care for her safety pissed him off. He'd have to make sure she understood just how dangerous her position could be if he weren't the one in control.

One stride put her lithe body inches from his, and even on tiptoe, he towered over her. Her lashes fluttered again, and her lips parted as if she hadn't expected his sudden move. She looked up at him as his hands settled on her waist then slipped around her to caress the silken skin of her back.

"You're mine." Holding her steady with one arm, he grabbed hold of her long ponytail and slowly wound it around his hand. When he'd reached the band at her scalp, he gave a slight tug. "Right now, you're mine. To do with as I want. Do you understand?"

"Yes." The word warmed his lips in a hushed whisper. Her nostrils flared.

"I don't think you do." He used his grip in her hair to force her head back. She sucked in a sharp breath but held his gaze, a spark of arousal lighting in those dark depths. He trailed the hand at the base of her spine up her ribs and around to fill his palm with her breast before traveling onward to splay at her throat. "I could strangle the life right out of you, and you couldn't do a thing to stop me."

Her body tensed, and the heat in her eyes dimmed. "Why are—"

"I could cut you to ribbons, and no one would hear you scream out here."

The muscles in her face relaxed, and her lips curved up in a knowing smile. "Ev, I'm not stupid. I learned my lesson." She wrapped one leg around his, hooked her heel at the back of his knee, and rubbed her pussy against his thigh. "I'm here to learn other things."

Moisture soaked through his jeans and warmed his skin, diffusing his anger and reminding him he was also here for other things. Things that would sate the relentless hunger he'd denied himself for the past few months. Still…

He ignored the pulsing in his cock and tightened his hand around her throat, not enough to cut off air but enough to get his point across. "You were sure quick to let me tie you up."

Again, she only smiled. "Because I trust you."

"Good. Trust is an important part of BDSM. But you shouldn't trust me. You haven't seen me in nine years. A person can change a lot in much less time."

A dark brow arched, revealing a hint of impatience. "Are you going to strangle or cut me? Or are you going to lecture me to death?"

He sighed and shook his head but couldn't stop the grin from taking the place of his frown. "No, no breath or knife play. That's not my thing."

She hugged his thigh tighter and strained against his grip on her hair. "Then tell me what is."

"I'd rather show you." He ground his hips into hers, letting her feel the hard length of his dick. "But first, promise me you'll never put yourself in this position with someone you haven't checked out."

"I won't."

"Say it."

She stared him straight in the eye. "I promise never to do this with someone I don't know and trust. Happy now?"

"Not as happy as I'm going to make you." He lowered his mouth to hers and leisurely tasted her lips with his tongue. Sweet. A hint of melon. Melon she'd shared with Josh. He wanted to punish her for that.

"Before we start, you should have a safeword." He nibbled at her lip. "If anything happens that you don't like or you're unsure of, say the word and I'll stop."

"What if I just have a question?"

"Okay then, we'll go with the standard safewords. Green is go; you're good. Yellow is for when you're uncertain or have a question that can't wait, though I'd rather you trust me to take care of you and save your curiosity for later. Red is for stop, a hard no, for when something is beyond what you're willing to endure."

"Traffic lights. Got it."

Easing back, Evan unwound her hair from his hand. He twirled her to face the opposite direction, wrapped his arm around her waist, and yanked her against his chest. The rope twanged like a plucked guitar. "As I said, trust is an important part of a D/s relationship."

The band holding her hair gave way to his fingers, and a cascade of chocolate waves flowed down her back. He buried his face in the silky softness and inhaled the vanilla fragrance of her shampoo.

"So do you go to one of these BDSM clubs?"

"Yes." He nuzzled the shell of her ear and let his hands wander the curves of her body. The sides of her ribs. The swell of her hips. The velvety plane of her stomach. He filled his palms with her heavy breasts and nipped at her earlobe.

Her head lolled backward to rest on his shoulder, baring the side of her neck for his pleasure. And by the moan vibrating against his lips as he closed his mouth over the ivory flesh beneath her ear and sucked hard, *her* pleasure as well.

"Do you like to watch others at your club? Having sex?" The question came out in a breathy sigh. "Like you did that night?"

His balls drew close to his body and pre-cum wet the fly of his jeans. He slid a hand down, reversing the path it had taken moments ago, stopping at the nearly bare mound between her legs. Her breath hitched, but she didn't move otherwise. He waited, drawing out the anticipation, then teased little circles in the dark curls above the crease of her folds.

"Yes, I like to watch. It's a large part of what I do." Dipping farther into the slick groove, he continued the slow circular pattern just above her engorged clit. He could make her come so easily. "Every time I think of your mouth around Tucker's dick, I get hard. And when I fuck you later, that's what I'll think about. Your pink lips glistening, cheeks sunken in against his cock as it reached for the back of your throat."

He dragged his finger from her pussy and slid it past her open lips into her hot mouth. "Suck my finger like you sucked his dick."

The searing suction around his finger, combined with the velvety roughness of her tongue, sent a jolt of electric pleasure straight to his cock. He shoved his hips against the small of her back. Another drop of pre-cum trickled down the throbbing shaft. "I can't wait to taste you."

Her whimper struck deep, unfurling the constriction around his chest, but her mewling sounds were only a tiny morsel to tease his palate and whet his appetite for more. He couldn't wait to devour her.

****

A delicious ache threaded through Shayna's arms, stretched taut above her head. Her hair sifted over her face as the warm breeze slipped under the low-hanging branches of the willow. Her entire body pulsed with need as Evan drew his finger from her mouth and swirled the wetness around her nipple.

So far, he'd done more talking than anything sexual, though somehow the talking had amped up her desire. So much so that her thighs were slick with it. She wanted him to fuck her, hard and fast, but she'd settle for his tongue if it meant release. She was that close to coming. "I'm hearing lots of talk. Where's the follow through?"

A chuckle rumbled from his chest and into her back, and his hands fell away from her breasts, his solid frame from her body. She heard him rummaging through the bag and wondered what torture device he'd use next.

The answer came as he knelt in front of her,

another set of cuffs in his hands, these larger than the ones on her wrists. He fit one around her left thigh, just above the knee, then another around the right. Whatever they were for, she liked the way they felt—strange, binding, sexy.

Before she could ask what he planned next, he stood and wrapped something around her midsection that looked like a corset with three silver rings on each side, one at the top, middle, and bottom. She'd seen it when she examined the bag earlier and hoped it wasn't something he'd wear himself.

A giggle bubbled inside her throat, and curiosity finally overpowered sexual excitement. She had to know. "What's that for?"

"I'm testing a theory." He yanked on the laces, drawing the contraption snug under her breasts and around her ribs. The black canvas, lined with sheepskin just like the cuffs, stopped an inch below her hipbones.

All amusement faded, and once again, she felt sexy, like a Victorian virgin held captive by a pirate. Yes, and she wanted to be his sex slave. Maybe there was more to this BDSM stuff than she thought. "What theory?"

"I'll tell you after I know the results." He went back to his bag and returned with another rope, same as the first only longer by the bulk of it.

The rope slipped easily through his hands as

he coiled it on the blanket at his feet. He'd done this many times. His actions were precise, practiced, confident. A small thrill rippled over her skin. Part of it was not knowing what he'd do with the rope. Another part was knowing it didn't matter. Whatever he did would feel good.

One end of the rope slithered through the ring on the cuff around her right thigh. He secured it in an intricate but sturdy looking knot. Tossing the other end over the limb above, he snaked it through the loop on the corset at her right hip. Again, over the branch and through the next ring. The process continued up the right side and down the left, first the limb, then the ring until the rope slipped through the last one on her left thigh.

She angled to look at him. "I'm starting to feel like a puppet."

His hands stilled, and his stormy blue eyes met hers. Oh, he was hot. Lusty hot. Obviously, this rope trick really turned him on.

"I guess you could say I'm your puppet master." He threw the rope over an adjacent branch and tugged it taut. Then he put his weight behind the next pull, and her left foot lifted off the ground. Another hard haul and her knee leveled with her breast.

"Oh." The movement startled her, but she began to understand where he was going with all this. With her leg hiked high, her pussy was exposed and almost the perfect height for him to fuck her standing up. Her inner muscles clamped down, and moisture seeped from her slit and along the crease of her ass to her anus.

Shayna didn't mind the tedious process of him adjusting and readjusting the tension and balance. Not one bit. Watching his muscles bunch and flex as he worked, envying the beads of sweat on his bronzed skin as they trailed over his pecs and jumped on the rollercoaster ride over his abs. That alone was enough to keep her happy. She only wished she were free to lick up the droplets as they reached the waistband of his jeans.

And the intensity on his beautiful face…

Damn, he made her pussy twitch.

Then there was the contraption itself. The sense of weightlessness, of not being able to move, the fact that she was helpless and at his mercy… She groaned and let her head drop back between her arms.

For the first time in the fifteen minutes it took him to get her exactly how he wanted her, Evan touched her, clasping her ankles with a firm grip to stop the motion. "You okay?"

"Mmm, yes." Actually, she would have thought her arms would hurt, but with other parts of her body taking her weight, she was quite comfortable. Almost as if she were in a hammock.

"One more thing." His hands drifted up her

shins and clamped around her knees. The pressure was brief and not nearly hard enough. Then he was gone again.

Frustration built as he came into view. With her head dangling backward, she was able to see him digging through his magic bag again. Seriously? What more could he do to her before he actually got down to the business of doing something to her?

Retrieving a black metal bar, he expanded it, then retracted it to about a foot and a half. He nodded his satisfaction and disappeared from view again.

Shayna lifted her head to find him between her legs. The bar had clasps at each end. "What's that?"

"A spreader bar." He connected one clasp to the ring on her right thigh cuff, pried her legs farther open, and latched the other end to the left cuff. Stepping back, he surveyed his handy work with a heated look. If she felt exposed before, now she was more so.

She rested her head against her arm and sighed. "This is a lot of work to go through when you could have just held me down."

"You won't be saying that when I'm done." His gaze locked on her open and vulnerable pussy. "And as wet as you are, I'd say you like the way it feels, being immobile, with no control over your body. Having no choice but to accept the pleasure—or the pain—I choose to give. Or not."

His words struck home. She more than liked it. As he'd worked, she'd liked it, as he said, but hearing him put into words what he planned or didn't plan skyrocketed desire to every nerve ending. Her breath shortened, and her fingers fumbled for a grip on the chain. Something tangible to hold on to, to focus on when no other part of her body found purchase. "So now what?"

"Now I take my turn." He sank to his knees, his face inches from her pussy. His strong hands palmed the inside of her thighs, thumbs prying the sensitive folds apart.

On instinct, Shayna tried to close her legs but couldn't. The bar kept them spread wide. Not that she wanted to keep him from his intent. She welcomed his mouth on her clit, his tongue in her channel. But fighting him made the surrender all the sweeter.

His laugh warmed the flesh above her folds, the only warning as his golden head lowered and his lips closed over her hard pulsing kernel. Her hips tried to buck, but she floundered. He held her steady and continued his assault, sucking, nipping, lapping circles. A delicious pressure coiled deep in the pit of her belly. Almost there.

His tongue shifted lower, stalling the orgasm as he laved the bare lips surrounding the clit he'd deserted. He raised his head slightly, his mouth barely teasing her skin. "You will not come. Do you understand?"

Through half open eyes, she glared at him. "Isn't that the whole purpose of this?"

His face remained stern, commanding. "The purpose is for me to decide. You're mine. I control when you come, when you don't. You'll obey or suffer punishment."

Shayna swallowed the retort forming on her lips. She wasn't sure where Evan had gone and who the man was taking his place, but she rather liked him. And the dark promise in his voice. Punishment? Yeah, she liked the sound of that, too. "Yes, Master."

"You say that with sarcasm now, but by the time I'm done, darlin', you'll say that with respect and gratitude." He slapped her bottom to demonstrate, and heat sifted into her flesh and wove its way to her core.

Biting her lip didn't stop the moan or the clutching of her inner muscles.

Another chuckle registered against her slit, then his tongue darted deep, curling to draw her juices, grazing the sensitive tissue of her inner walls. His hands roamed to cup her ass, and his fingers dug into her cheeks.

Pain. Oh god, the pain. Sweet, unbearable, exquisite, torturous. "Yes."

That marvelous tongue withdrew, depriving her once again of the orgasm he drove her toward. The wet tip circled her anus. She flinched, surprised that he'd gone there. Merciless fingers spread her cheeks before she could decide whether she wanted him there or not, and his tongue speared deeper, rimming the tight ring.

Rapture. Molten lava. That was the only way to describe the feel of his penetration. Rapturous molten lava oozing through every vein. An orgasm, unique from any other orgasm she'd ever known, caught her in its slow-moving current.

As the pleasure drifted to a halt, his tongue stilled. "Naughty girl. You disobeyed."

He licked a path upward, gathering her juices. She tried to twist away, but his teeth grazed her over-stimulated clit and another orgasm ripped from her center. She shrieked, and her toes curled, yet the bliss was short lived, not enough to satisfy.

The flat of his tongue lapped once more from back to front, then he sat back on his heels. "That's twice."

She could barely breathe or hold her head up, but she managed to open her eyes and shoot him a look she hoped contained daggers. "If you don't want me to come, then don't do things like that."

Standing, he loomed over her, his face a mask of indifference. "You'll learn the longer you hold out, the longer you fight it, the more intense the orgasm."

"Is that what you're doing? Holding out?"

Now he smiled. "Yes."

His hand reached for the button at the waistband of his jeans. It gave way easily, happily, if jeans could be happy about being shed to allow their wearers to have sex. The zipper was just as delighted to oblige, the whirring sound like a sigh of worship.

You're losing it, totally losing it.

The denim fly gaped, and the head of his long, thick erection peeked out. He shoved the jeans down to reveal the shaft, the skin taut, ropey veins threading from tip to base and disappearing in a thatch of golden-brown hair. His heavy sac hung low. The sight was familiar but much hotter than she remembered. And last night had been too dark to appreciate him fully.

"You can expect punishment later for both transgressions." He stepped out of his jeans, kicked them aside, and sheathed his cock with a condom she hadn't seen him take from…his wallet? Back pocket?

And what had he said? Punishment? What kind? Who cared when both orgasms had been delicious and worth any penance he doled out? Hell, she'd probably enjoy it.

She swayed her hips as much as the ropes would allow. "Bring it on."

Chapter Seven

Evan wasn't sure if he wanted to kiss that smart mouth or fuck it. His dick jerked, eager to fuck something—Shayna's mouth, her pussy, her ass. He groaned and moved closer, placing his cock at her juicy entrance. Her mouth and ass could wait for another time. This was about her and testing his theory.

The soft pale flesh of her hips yielded to his grip as he slowly drew her toward him in the makeshift sling. The mouth of her tight cunt gave way to the head of his cock. She made that little noise that sounded like a purr, and her pussy locked around his shaft. He struggled for a breath, inhaled the scent of her sex, and fought the urge to slam deep and hard.

Testing a theory. Testing a theory.

Grinding his teeth, he eased her another inch down his shaft. The site of his wide girth stretching the mouth of her pussy, seeing her cunt swallow him, convulsively working to take him deeper… Fucking hot.

Halfway in, he swung her away, totally withdrawing. She whimpered, feeding the ravenous hunger inside him. He needed to hear how much she wanted him to fuck her. For her to know he could withhold pleasure at whim and make her plead for it.

He rocked her toward him again, then quickly away, popping his crown in and out, savoring the tight squeeze around the sensitive ridge. Back and forth, back and forth.

"Ev…ahh, yes."

"Don't come." Dragging his gaze from their joined parts to her face, he stopped on an out-stroke.

"No, don't stop!" She tried to squirm closer, but he dug his fingers into her hips.

"Don't you dare come." If she came again, he'd be lost. He'd lose control. That didn't happen. Not since he'd trained as a Dom. What was it about Shayna that drove him to the brink of sanity? "Breathe."

The last command was more for himself than for her. But the deeper he breathed, the more he wanted to pound into her. He was kidding himself if he thought this session could last much longer.

He closed his eyes to the vision of Shayna's slender body bound for his pleasure and tried to think of something else. Something besides how fast his heart thumped against his chest, how the hot velvety glove of her pussy fisted around his dick as he leisurely sheathed himself.

The bar between her thighs bumped his chest, tilting her hips upward as he pushed against it. The farther he slid, the more her knees pressed toward her shoulders and the deeper his cock drove. When his balls mashed against her ass, he paused.

"God, Evan, please fuck me. Fuck me hard."

Her plea melted over him, tempting him to give in. Fuck, he wanted to…badly. His cock twitched, begging him. No, not this time. Next time, he'd fuck her hard until she screamed but…

Teeth grinding as his control threatened to crack, he stiffened the muscles in his ass to keep from thrusting and dragged her onto his shaft and then off. Back and forth. On and off. Tight. Hot. Squeezing. Pressure.

With every measured inhale and exhale, with every gentle rock of her hips, every incredible sucking grasp of her pussy, the higher his balls rose. The familiar crackle of electricity sparked in his lower spine. He needed to come.

Evan opened his eyes, filling his brain with Shayna—bound, flushed, head craned back, lips parted. Sweat beaded her forehead and drizzled into damp strands of silken hair that reached for the ground. Her fingers clutched the chain between the cuffs, knuckles white. The muscles in her upper arms and shoulders etched through translucent skin as she strained to lift her body to take him, a wasted effort, but one that gave him immense pleasure.

His gaze zeroed in on plump, pink nipples topping creamy tits that bounced above the black corset to the tempo of the rocking motion. He slid his hands along her sides, over her breasts. Leaning over her, his chest shoved the bar and her knees closer to her body. His cock slipped deeper, and their simultaneous moans startled a bird from its nest above.

Fuck, he needed to come. He needed her to come first.

He bent his knees and continued the deliberate thrusts, the new angle driving the head of his cock against the upper wall of her cunt. She gasped as the ridge around his crown scraped her G-spot. At the same time, he squeezed and rolled her nipple.

A stifled scream rent the air, followed by a racking sob, both sweet music to his ears. Her pussy clamped hard around his shaft, resisting the in-and-out lunges. Rolling spasms milked his cock. He couldn't hang on.

Heat sizzled from his balls, pulsing through his shaft. Cum jetted in waves into the condom as he pumped through the forceful orgasm. Four, five, six…seven times until the last drop was spent and he stilled, savoring the tiny aftershocks fluttering through her and into him.

He didn't want to move, but Shayna would lose feeling in her arms and legs if he didn't. She murmured her discomfort—or was it dismay?—when he straightened, took hold of her hips, and eased his partially hard dick from her still-quaking pussy. He disposed of the condom, then quickly donned his jeans, not bothering to zip or button them in his hurry to get her down.

The knot slipped free easily, but he kept a firm grip and let the slack out slowly, making her descent gradual. Her head lolled, her body limp. To anyone else wandering on the scene, they'd have thought her dead or injured. To Evan, he'd done his job as her Dom. He'd coaxed her body to extreme euphoric pleasure.

When her feet touched the ground, he lowered her until she lay on the blanket. He removed the spreader bar, corset, and cuffs and hauled her onto his lap. Brushing the hair from her face, he massaged the reddened flesh where the cuffs had been, marks that only stirred a primal lust to create more.

He kissed the top of her head. "Shay? You okay?"

A long, drawn-out sigh whispered across his chest. "Mmm, better than okay." She tilted her head back to look up at him. "How do you do that?"

He chuckled and reached behind him for her

dress. "Do what?"

"Make me come so freakin' hard."

"Glad to know I didn't disappoint." He motioned with the garment for her to let him dress her, and she held her arms above her head. "We'll talk about it later. You should be getting back."

A yawn sounded from behind the material as he tugged it over her head and down to her waist. "What time is it?"

"I don't know." He glanced at the sun on the west side of the lake now. "Probably around three-thirty or four."

Her dark eyes widened, and she scrambled off his lap to find her sandals. "Crap. I didn't expect to be gone that long. Josh will be hungry in another hour, and I don't have anything prepared for supper."

Josh will be hungry. Frowning, Evan leaned back on one elbow and watched her hop from one foot to the other to slip on her shoes. He'd just given her three orgasms—freakin' hard orgasms by her admission—and she was worried about Josh's fucking dinner. "Hey, I'm the one who just worked up an appetite."

Second shoe in place, she stood over him, a big grin on her face. With a quick twist of her wrist, her hair was back in a ponytail. How she found the band for it, he wasn't sure.

She planted a foot on the other side of his hip

and lowered herself to straddle him. Her hands landed on his chest and pushed him to his back. She leaned forward, the heat from her pussy filtering through his open fly, her mouth hovering above his. "I have a feeling I could never satisfy your appetite. But I'm willing to try. I'll be your dessert tonight."

She lowered her head to kiss him, but he grabbed her ponytail and kept her lips from meeting his. "You might be right about that. And if you kiss me, dessert will come before dinner and you won't make it back before dark."

A tremor shimmied through her body, and her lashes fluttered. He could read the indecision in those dark eyes. She wanted him again, but she had a job to do. Fuck Josh. Evan wanted her to choose him.

Her eyes shut tight, and she pushed against his chest. "I gotta go."

He released her hair and sat up, lifting her off his crotch and to her feet. "Just leave everything. I'll get it."

She blinked, obviously surprised and a little confused by his harsh tone. No more than he was. He couldn't take his disappointment out on her. She was getting paid to take care of Josh's needs, not his.

Rising, he crowded into her space, tipped her head back, and smiled to reassure her. "I'll be right behind you."

She didn't quite look convinced, but she nodded and turned to go.

He caught her wrist. "Shay?"

Her lips thinned as she tucked them between her teeth and stared at his chest. "Hmm?"

What the hell? Was that a hint of hurt in her eyes?

Damn, if he wasn't careful, he'd screw this up. "You can expect your punishment tonight." He slapped her ass and gave her a little nudge. "Think about that while you're making dinner."

Her eyelids fluttered faster. Her cheeks grew flushed. But the smile he'd hoped for returned.

She trotted up the hill to his pickup. He liked seeing her behind the wheel of his truck. Something about it made him feel warm.

Fuck, what was that about? Had to be the sudden unleashing of his pent-up dominant side. Providing for her needs, that was it. He couldn't afford anything more than that.

But for the first time in six months, the ropes around Evan's chest had loosened. They'd grow tight again eventually, but at least they weren't suffocating him anymore.

He should have found a new partner ages ago. As much as he loved Clay and Lindsey, he wouldn't survive much longer in the less-dominant role. He'd needed today. In more ways than one.

He felt whole again. He had put the pain of his past with Shayna to rest. There was no guilt, other than for leaving without talking to her. The ghosts were gone. Some of them anyway. He couldn't afford to let the ones still roaming the empty chambers of his heart into his head. Loving Shayna again was not an option.

He picked up the rope and began winding it around his shoulder and elbow. He had things to do that didn't call for standing around like a lovesick pup. He had the results of his experiment to relay and punishment to administer. He wasn't quite sure which he looked forward to most.

His cock pulsed in answer.

Fuck, yeah, the punishment.

****

The twang of the spring on the screen door set Shayna's nerves in a tizzy. She glanced over her shoulder, expecting Evan's tall frame to fill the space just inside the kitchen. He'd said he would be right behind her.

But Rusty stood on the mat, hat in hand, his wiry cowboy build thin enough that a strong gust could topple him. White hair stuck to his partially bald head, and a worried frown cut grooves in his already wrinkled brow. "You seen Josh?"

"Not this afternoon." She'd hurried through a

quick shower and got right to work on supper. "You can check the den."

"Yes, ma'am. Thanks." He ambled into the hall.

Ground turkey stuck to her palms as she rolled another ball and smashed it on the cutting board. *Great nurse you are.*

She should have checked on Josh first thing. But the thought of facing him, knowing he knew what she'd been doing with Evan… Heat rushed over her skin, and she clenched her thighs under the filmy print skirt.

And she was still a bit shaken by Evan's behavior before she'd left. He was upset with her, though she had no idea what she'd done wrong. Oh, he'd tried to cover up his flash of irritation with the teasing threat of punishment. But she'd seen it.

Way to go, Shayna. Ruin the best sexual encounter in forever.

The screen door squeaked again and banged against the frame, making her jump. She swiveled around this time to find the youngest hand searching the room. "Mr. McNamara around?"

"Which one?"

He laughed. "Evan. Thought I saw him headed to the house."

Shit. Had he walked right past her? "I haven't seen—"

Again, the screen door protested. Her heart skipped a beat, and her stomach flipped as Evan sauntered in, all broad shoulders, long legs, a looming tower of gorgeous masculinity. He eyed Mark, then hung up his hat and strolled past her to the sink, his hand brushing her waist.

Turning on the faucet, his stormy gaze clashed with hers for a brief instant, then shifted beyond her. "Mark?"

"Just wanted to thank you."

Shayna ducked her head and concentrated on forming another turkey burger with trembling hands. Her breath caught, her breasts tingled and grew heavy under the lace bra, and now she couldn't breathe at all. Oh god, he was hungry again.

From the corner of her eye, she saw him squirt soap on those magical hands and lather them up. She nearly moaned thinking about them sudsing her up in the shower, the palms of his hands sliding over her aching nipples—

"For what?"

Her head snapped up at his gruff voice. He was checking out the cleavage exposed by the low-cut T-shirt she'd chosen for just that purpose. She ducked her head and went back to work.

"Cari," Mark said. "She said yes."

"Did you expect her to say otherwise?"

The boy laughed, his happiness refusing to be

daunted by Evan's curt tone. "No, sir."

"Well, there you go." Evan tore a paper towel from the rack under the cabinet and settled a hip against the counter so close to her she could feel his warmth.

"She wanted to know why I didn't wait 'til she graduated like we'd talked about."

Evan grunted. Really, he was being beyond rude.

Shayna glanced at Mark. The boy was chomping at the bit to share his moment in the sun with someone. "So what did you tell her?"

He grinned from ear to ear. "I told her what Mr. McNamara said. That life is short, love is hard to come by, and sometimes, a man just needs to claim what's his."

"I see." She turned an is-that-so look on the man beside her.

Evan just shrugged and chucked the wadded-up towel over the table and into the waste basket.

"Well, just wanted to come say thanks for the advice."

"Congratulations, Mark." She elbowed Evan.

He grunted again but pushed off the counter and met Mark with an outstretched hand. "Congratulations, man. Why don't you take off early to celebrate with friends?"

"Thanks, but most of my friends think I'm

crazy getting tied down to one woman. Cal invited me over for dinner though. His wife is fixin' up my favorite, pork chops and fried cabbage."

"Mmm, sounds good." Evan opened the back door and held it for Mark. What was his problem? "Better get going before Shayna makes you eat a turkey burger."

Her mouth fell open. "What's wrong with turkey burgers?"

Mark rubbed his flat belly and backed his way toward the door. "Nothing at all, ma'am. But I have a hard enough time keeping the weight on."

"Hmph." She gathered another handful from the bowl.

The screen door had barely slammed shut when Evan's arms snaked around her waist. One hand splayed on the flat of her belly. The other cupped her breast and squeezed. His hips pressed into her back. He ground his erection into her ass, his nose tickling her ear. "I thought he'd never leave."

"Is that why you were so mean?"

He chuckled, and his warm breath teased her skin. "Was I mean?"

With a will of its own, her body melted into him as his lips opened on the curve of her neck. "As if you didn't know."

"Sometimes a man just wants to claim what's

his." His hand on her breast tightened. "And right now, you're mine."

There was that qualifier again. He'd said the same this afternoon. *Right now.* Not later. Probably not tomorrow. And for sure not in the future, when she no longer worked for Josh. Just right now.

It was enough. What other choice did she have?

What other choice do you want?

She swallowed the sudden lump in her throat and steeled herself against the foolish emotions bubbling in her chest. She could do right now. It was enough. "Yes, I'm yours."

"Meet me in my room in fifteen minutes."

He literally meant right now.

Shayna looked at her hands covered with yuck. She still had burgers to cook and had yet to cut up the sweet potatoes. They'd take at least a half hour to bake. "I can't possibly—"

"You will." The command wasn't sharp, but the quiet strength held a dark promise of reckoning should she refuse. And a hint of the displeasure she'd caught earlier. "It's time for your punishment."

"Right now?" Well, of course. Hadn't he just said that? "I mean, I thought you'd wait until after we ate."

"You thought wrong." He relaxed his hold and eased away except for his hands at her waist. "Fifteen minutes, Shayna. Don't make me come looking for you."

With that warning, he left her standing there, one big hot mess and no time to think about what he had planned. Or what the hell she'd tell Josh about why dinner was late. It took her three minutes to get the patties finished, wrapped in foil, and stashed in the fridge. Another ten to peel and cut the potatoes. At least that much would be done. She washed her hand and made a mad dash down the hall.

"Oh." She plowed into Rusty as he exited the den. He righted her before she fell against the wall. Her hand flew to her throat, and she edged toward the stairs. "Sorry about that."

"No harm done." He tipped his hat. "Night, ma'am."

"Shayna, is that you?" Josh hollered from behind Rusty.

"Can't talk right now." Guilt assailed her, but the rush of exhilaration over what was to come made it seem inconsequential. Heart pounding, she raced up the stairs and topped the landing as the bathroom door opened. A squeak escaped her, and she darted down the hall and into Evan's room just ahead of him with a few seconds to spare. "Made it."

"So you did." The towel on his hips outlined his approval even if his voice didn't.

She bent at the waist, her hands on her knees, and tried to catch her breath. "I think you wanted me to be late." Probably hoped she'd add to her mounting infractions.

"The fact that you barely made it tells me something other than my instructions were a priority for you." He wandered to a chest of drawers and opened a box. "Take off your clothes."

His disapproval was palpable. She hadn't realized how important her compliance was to him. She'd thought it a game. Straightening, she fingered the hem of her shirt and silently stripped it over her head. Her bra landed on top of her shirt on the floor. She wanted him to look at her, but he donned a pair of jeans sans underwear.

"Ev?" Why was he dressing if he wanted her to undress? Had he changed his mind? Her stomach twisted at the thought.

When he didn't answer or glance her way, she unzipped her skirt and slid it over her hips. She stepped out of the flowery print pooled at her feet and left her flip-flops behind. She hadn't worn panties, hoping he'd like that as he had when she'd stripped earlier. Still, he didn't acknowledge her. "Ev? I'm sorry."

He looked at her then, his hard blue eyes

softening. He sighed. "No, I'm sorry." He moved to stand in front of her. "This is a way of life for me, Shay. I expect my submissive to be eager to please me. But you can't know that, therefore I can't fault you."

His disappointment in her lack of knowledge and experience hurt. She did want to please him. She just didn't know how. "You want me to be submissive to you?"

"It's not a matter of me wanting you to, although I do. The fact is you are, by nature, a sub. You might not realize it, but you crave dominance."

"I don't think so." She was independent and hated being told what to do, especially by some overbearing male who thought he knew what was best for her. Women who looked to a man to make decisions for them were weak, and she didn't understand them at all. "No, I respect myself too much for that."

He smiled. "I'm talking about sexual dominance."

"Yes, of course." *You say that like you understand what he's talking about.* "Was this part of your theory testing?"

"Yes." He circled her to sit on the bed. "Come here."

As she drew near, he clasped her hips and maneuvered her between his legs. His mouth covered one nipple, sucking hard. She gasped as pleasure rippled from her breast to her core. She watched his face as he drew her deeper into his mouth. Eyes closed, dark golden lashes fanning cheekbones. His jaw, freshly shaven, worked as he tongued her flesh. Straight white teeth nipped and tugged on the nipple.

Her clit zinged, and her pussy quivered. She drove her fingers into the soft blond waves and tried to pull his mouth closer. Strong fingers encircled her wrists and squeezed hard enough to force her to let go.

He guided her hands behind her back. "Lock your hands around your wrists and keep them there until I say otherwise."

She did as he said, and the position thrust her breasts up and out. His tongue laved the nipple he'd been toying with before he slipped a small metal square around it. Then he turned what looked like screws on each side that gripped her nipple in a tight vise.

A jagged arc of pain ripped down the same path the pleasure had taken, initiating a deliciously forbidden ecstasy. "Oh my."

"Yes, you also like your pain, don't you?"

Her head spinning, Shayna gazed into his hot, lust-filled eyes. "Mmmhmm."

"But I want you to think back on our afternoon. Did I give you any pain?"

Other than the sting of her scalp when he pulled at her hair, the slight friction around her wrists, and the sweet torture of prolonging her orgasm, no, he hadn't dealt her any pain. Not like this. "No."

"And yet you came." His lips latched onto her other nipple, mashing it to the roof of his mouth with his tongue.

"Mmm, yes." Her pussy muscles twitched, and moisture slickened her thighs. She wiggled to create friction where she needed it.

His tongue sketched wet circles around the areola. "You came hard. *Freakin'* hard as I recall."

She wanted him to stop talking and suck her tit. She struggled not to use her hands to force the issue. But he seemed to be going somewhere with the discussion, so she ground her teeth and waited for him to continue.

"And I wasn't rough with you?"

"No." In fact, he'd been strongly gentle if that was possible.

"I can give you rough, Shay, if that's what you want." More tongue smoothing, lifting, teasing. "But I don't think it's what you need to find release."

"Back to your theory, are we?" Frustration seethed within her, and again, she fought the urge to grab a handful of his hair and make him suck. Better yet, she could pinch the damn nipple herself. Instead, she dug her fingernails into her forearms to keep from letting go and shuddered at the sharp sensation.

Ha! She could have pleasure *and* obey.

"What you get off on is the restraint," he said. "You like being held down. You said it yourself. And today, you liked the cuffs, the immobility. You liked knowing I was in control and you were helpless to stop me from doing whatever I wanted to you."

God, yes.

"Let me teach you." He nipped at the tender flesh on the underside of her breast. "Let me show you the pleasure of submission."

"Yes, please."

She sighed when he answered by closing his mouth around her nipple and drawing hard. His teeth snagged her nipple and pulled, then slowly dragged the elongated bud through the razor-sharp edges. She caught her bottom lip between her teeth to stifle the moan.

"Don't hold back, Shay. I want to hear your pleasure." He'd said as much earlier today but…

"The door's open." She hissed in a breath as he tweaked the nipple and slid on another ring. "Josh might hear."

Evan paused, and the look on his face said she'd somehow displeased him again. Then the screws tightened, wielding a subtler pain than the first. More fluid seeped from her core.

When he'd finished, he planted his hands on her hips. "He knows what we're doing. Not this minute, but he knew what you came to the lake for."

"I know." A rush of heat blazed from the roots of her hair to her toes.

"Does it bother you that he knows? I'm pretty sure he expected this to happen."

"No, and I'm pretty sure he not only expected it but planned this whole thing to *make* it happen. Not the broken bones, but you and I being here." At least that was the impression Josh had given her this morning. "But it's one thing him knowing. Another that he's listening. I'm just not used to being that…out there."

His gaze flared hotter. "You didn't seem to mind that night with Tucker."

The memory of that identical gaze watching her blow Tucker made her squirm. "That's not fair. I was more than a little intoxicated at the time."

"There are ways to feel that same intoxication without alcohol."

Yes, yes, a thousand times yes. She wanted that feeling, wanted to dwell in that euphoric state for hours on end. "Show me."

"I will. I promise. But first, you have to know what happens when you disobey." Evan backed her up and turned her to face the bed. "Kneel on the edge of the mattress."

Oh, hell. Was he going to spank her? She'd never been spanked, but if that punishment came at Evan's hand, she'd probably like it. He seemed to know exactly what she needed.

"Keep your hands behind your back." He helped hold her steady as she wobbled to find balance on the bed. He thrust his knee between her thighs and nudged them farther apart. "Now bend forward."

Again, she counted on Evan to keep her from face planting into the bed. When her forehead met the mattress, he pressed her chest to the sheet, causing her back to arch. She turned her head to the side and tried to look over her shoulder, but her position didn't allow for that.

His hands traveled down to her neck and shoulders, applying an easy pressure, then roamed leisurely up her spine until they paused on the globes of her ass. "Did you enjoy having your ass rimmed today?"

She'd never heard the term, but if he meant having his tongue spear her hole... Her anus folded in on itself, then blossomed, eager for his wet penetration, and damn if she didn't wiggle her ass like a cat ready for her tom. What? Now she was an anal slut? "You know I did."

"Then I think you'll like this."

The squirting sound registered a second before something cold dripped into the crease of her ass. He smeared what had to be lube down and around the rosette. His fingertip zeroed in on the center and screwed its way to the first knuckle.

The sensation was like no other. Warming, tingling, humming, electrifying, glorious, and at the same time dark, forbidden, decadent… There weren't enough ways to describe it. Who cared? As long as it didn't stop.

She shoved back, needing more.

"Easy. Not too fast."

That made her laugh. "Shouldn't I be the one saying that?"

He grunted and slid his finger deeper, pressing against the sensitive tissue and eliciting more of the dark, yummy, indescribable feelings. This punishment thing wasn't so bad if this was all he planned. She'd have all this naughty goodness and maybe an orgasm to top the one this afternoon.

Just when he'd lodged his finger all the way, he pulled out.

"Evan." The long, drawn-out whine of his name would have embarrassed her under normal circumstances, but this was most certainly not normal. Not for her.

A stinging slap on her ass cheek shocked her eyes wide open. It hurt like hell for a fraction of a moment, then heat bloomed into her core. Her entire body relaxed, and her eyelids flickered shut. No doubt about it. She'd enjoy a spanking.

Another squirt and then the prodding began again, two fingers this time, stretching her hole wider. The burn was greater, sweeter. He scissored his fingers, and a heady swirl of pure pleasure spun straight to her core.

"Uh, uh, uh." His fingers slid out, and she wanted to scream. "No orgasms for you."

What? Was he freakin' kidding?

"This is your punishment. Pleasure without fulfillment."

"No!" She twisted to look at him. "You can't—"

His palm met the same spot as before, harder though. "Be still."

The pleasure-pain was twice as delicious as the first swat, but she didn't have time to relish it. Something foreign and slightly broader than his two fingers probed the constricted opening and screwed its way past the tight ring of muscle. "Oh, god."

"Maybe next time you'll think twice about coming without permission."

And then again, maybe not. She rather liked the consequences, both the spanking and the screwing of her ass. But she wouldn't admit it to him. He'd probably come up with something that might really hurt, like… Was there anything he could do she wouldn't like? Probably not.

A formidable growl preceded more pressure. As the object inched deeper, it widened even more, sending a cascade of bliss over every nerve ending. Surely an orgasm was on the horizon. And what did she care if it gained her more of this?

"Jesus, Shay. I could come just watching you take this plug. And my dick wishes it could trade places." His voice sounded strained, his breathing labored. He was totally into what he was doing to her. That realization only spiked her closer to climax.

The butt plug—now that she knew what it was—stopped snug against her sphincter. Evan stepped to the end of the bed to wipe his hands on the towel he'd worn after his shower, then returned to gently remove the excess lube.

"Okay. You're all set. You can get dressed now."

Oh, no, no, no, no, no, no…no! He didn't just tell her they were done. Uh-uh.

"Hurry up. Dinner's late."

Shayna unlocked her hands and winced as she unfolded her arms a little too fast in an effort to push herself up on hands and knees and get turned around. "You can't be serious."

He tugged a clean, gray T-shirt over his head,

covering the scrumptious abs she'd want to lick if she weren't mad. Swiping her skirt off the floor, he handed it to her. "Come on. *Josh* is waiting."

The sarcasm in his voice didn't go unnoticed, though she couldn't begin to guess what he had to be pissed off about. She was the one with a plug up her ass and what felt like a mini-mammogram taking place on her nipples. She suffered a throbbing ache in her pussy from both.

She snatched the swatch of material from him, clutched it to her chest, and sat gingerly on the edge of the bed, aware of the fullness in her ass. "You're just going to leave me like this? You're not even going to take the edge off so I can think straight?"

He shrugged. "That's why they call it punishment."

Her mouth hung open in disbelief. He freakin' shrugged. As if he'd asked something of her as trivial as brushing her hair or wearing lipstick.

"Maybe next time I tell you not to come, you'll do as you're told." He grabbed her shirt and bra and waited for her to put on the skirt. "You'll wear the plug and clamps during dinner, and we'll see if you learn anything."

Shayna wanted to stamp her foot, but the simple act of rising to her feet sent a wave of hot sensation through her core. How would she make it through supper when her insides melted with every movement?

Oh, wait, I don't need him. She could curb this horny frustration with her vibrator before she went downstairs. Could even sneak back up for a little quickie if she had to. And he'd never know. She almost giggled at the deviousness of her rebellious plan.

"Fine." She eased her legs into the skirt and stood to yank it up. No need for him to know she wasn't angry anymore.

He held out her bra but when her fingers closed around the lace, he didn't let go. His gaze landed on her breasts.

"Wait." His expression flitted with indecision for a moment, then he tugged the garment from her grasp and held out the shirt. "No bra."

"Why?"

Tossing the bra on his bed, he closed the space between them. He lifted her against his chest. Her tummy did a little flip as her feet left the ground and his mouth slanted over to hers. His tongue dipped inside to brush hers briefly, retreated, and flickered in again.

She tried to coax him into a deeper kiss, but he pulled away and rested his forehead against hers. He closed his eyes tight, his jaw clenching hard, as if a great battle raged inside him.

When he opened his eyes, she swallowed. They burned into hers, just as they had that night so long ago. "Because I want to see the clamps through your shirt. I want to know they're weighing on your nipples. That when you move and your tits bounce, you'll feel the tug and cream will drip from your pussy."

With every word, her heart thumped faster. The air trying to fill her lungs met resistance as her breathing grew shallow. How could his dirty words arouse her to the point that he wouldn't have to wait for that cream to slide down her thighs?

He blew out a breath and eased her down his torso, said clamps dragging over the soft cotton of his T-shirt. "Now be a good girl and don't pout. It doesn't become you, Shay."

Stupidly, she shook her head. "I won't."

He shook a finger at her. "And don't even think about cheating with that little vibrator of yours. You won't find it where you left it."

"How did you—" She snapped her mouth shut.

"As long as we're in this, you will not self-pleasure unless I give you permission. Do you understand?"

Shayna nodded absently, and he gave her a nudge toward the door. A swat to her ass sent her scurrying through it, cramming her head and arms through her shirt. That only made her nipples zing and an odd but exhilarating pleasure zip through her ass. And with each step down the stairs, she zinged and zipped…and creamed some more.

It was going to be a very long and a very wet evening.

Chapter Eight

Evan smiled from behind the newspaper as Shayna paused mid-stride, shuddered, and moved on. She seemed to be dealing well with the plug and vises while she finished preparing supper. Better than he was.

Her punishment turned out to be his as well. After watching the plug slide into her ass, he'd been hard pressed not to cram her puffy pink cunt full of cock. Normally, the punishment he administered to a sub spiked his lust a notch but never to the point he struggled with control. That kiss to coax her into compliance had just about done him in. He'd come close to throwing her on the bed and fucking her hard and fast, to hell with teaching her a lesson.

He deserved to suffer right along with her. He'd failed at his job as her Dom. He'd failed to read the signs and pull back. He knew she was close and yet he'd let her come, needed her to. And here she was, paying the consequences. Still, a sub had to learn to obey her Dom.

Not that she wanted to be a sub.

You want her to want it. To want you as her

Master.

He resisted the idea. He might be a Dom, but he'd never been anyone's Master. Never collared anyone. Never even come close to wanting to.

Shayna would look good with a collar. His collar.

Fuck. He was venturing into dangerous territory. Thinking things he had no business thinking. She wanted sex, rough sex, and he'd offered to show her a world beyond that. End of story. Moving on.

Folding the newspaper, Evan adjusted his semi-erect cock and focused on something other than the arousal she tried to hide. "So, for a nurse, you're pretty efficient in the kitchen."

She bent to pull the fries out of the oven and groaned. "I have to eat, don't I?"

The testiness in her voice tugged at his lips, but he suppressed the smile. "I thought we agreed you wouldn't pout."

She sucked in a deep breath, blew it out, and the baking sheet didn't so much as clang as she carefully laid it on the stovetop with precision.

"I'm not pouting." Her tone had lost some of its bite but still carried an edge. "I'm freakin' horny."

He let his amusement show this time and leaned back in the chair. "If it's any consolation, you're not alone."

She smiled over her shoulder. "Good."

Semi-erect went to full blown hard-on with the sultriness of her smile and the heavy-lidded slant of her eyes. If Josh didn't show soon, Evan was afraid when he did, he'd walk in to find Shayna bent over the kitchen table and Evan pounding into her. Despite the jealousy gnawing at him, the idea hitched up his lust.

Moving on, remember?

"Tell me. Where did you learn to cook and why the healthy choices?"

"When Mom got sick"—she scraped the fries into a bowl—"one of the doctors said there were two things she'd seen help patients beat cancer, besides medical treatment. The power of positive thinking and a healthy diet. We did a lot of research and found that sticking to organic foods and a healthy diet made the whole family feel better."

He remembered Josh telling him about Shayna moving to Austin and the reason for it. That was when he stopped listening to his brother's not so subtle prattle. Hearing about her and the tough time she was going through only made him feel that much guiltier.

"I guess you live on preservatives, too, like Josh." She reached for the plates in the cabinet overhead and hissed in a breath. Her hands cupped her breasts, and the muscles in her back tensed.

"Supper ready?" Josh swung on his crutch into the kitchen.

Shayna lowered her hands to the counter and gripped the edge hard, knuckles turning white. "No, supper isn't ready."

Evan started to rise, but she seemed to recover as she turned and placed the plates on the table. Her shirt was more transparent that he'd thought and clung to her breasts, clearly outlining the vises around her nipples.

"Jesus." Josh's curse tore Evan's attention from the beautiful display that tied him in knots. His brother's mouth hung open, and his gaze was locked on Shayna's tits.

Cheeks flushed, she lifted her gaze to meet Josh's across the table. "Don't say a word."

Jealousy cut through Evan with a jagged blade as he watched the silent conversation passing between the two. He was starting to regret the punishment. Or rather making it so obvious to his brother. He and Shayna had a connection of some kind from the past that went beyond friendship. They might not have been lovers, but the thought was there on both sides. He would lay money on it.

Mine.

Evan stood abruptly, his chair screeching backward and drawing their startled focus to him.

He looked at Shayna and struggled to keep the rage coursing through him under control. "My office. Now."

"But supper—" She must have seen his jaw tighten because she nodded and quietly rose from her chair and exited the room.

As soon as she disappeared, Josh swung a heated gaze on Evan. "What the fuck, Ev?"

"This is between me and Shayna." Evan pushed in his chair. He barely understood what was driving him.

"But what the hell was she wearing?

"It's none of your business."

"How can you treat her like that? She's not one of your pets. But she'll do anything for you even if it's not what she wants."

Josh had never understood Evan's sexual appetites, and he never would so Evan didn't waste time explaining or trying to make him understand that Shayna needed more than the vanilla sex that Josh could offer.

He transferred the bowl of orange fries and a platter of beige meat patties to the table with a bang, then tossed Josh a sack of bread. "You know how to put a burger together, right?"

Josh caught the loaf with his good hand. "What's eating you?"

"She's mine. That's what's *eating* me." He

plunked a jar of mayonnaise on the table.

"I get that."

"Do you?" Before he could stop himself, he asked the question he already knew the answer to. "Can you deny your attraction to her?"

"Hey, I'm a man same as you." Josh grimaced. "Well, not exactly like you. But yeah, I think Shayna's hot, and if you weren't in the picture, I'd be all over that."

Evan braced both hands on the table and leaned toward his brother. "Well, I *am* here, and you will keep your eyes above her shoulders at all times. Got it?"

His brother held up both hands, only one allowing him to splay his hand in surrender. "Whatever you say."

Satisfied he'd made his point, Evan made his way to his office. It was time to make sure Shayna understood exactly who she belonged to.

****

Shayna paced the small office, waffling between anger for the way Evan had humiliated her in front of Josh and the lust stealing her breath and wetting her thighs every time she ran scenarios of what he'd do to her when he showed up. She hadn't done anything wrong. He had no right to treat her that way. On the other hand, she'd recognized the flare of jealousy in his eyes when Josh was staring at her breasts, and his reaction did funny things to her pussy…and her heart.

She jumped as Evan's large frame filled the doorway, his eyes as ice-blue as she'd ever seen them.

She pointed a finger at him. "You're the one who made me wear the damn things."

In two strides, he was in front of her, hands gripping her shoulders. "You're mine. Only mine."

"I'm—"

He laid a finger over her mouth and closed his eyes. His nostrils flared as he sucked in several deep breaths and exhaled slowly. Finally, he opened his eyes and pinned her with a gaze she couldn't read. "I'm going to ask you one more time. Is there something between you and Josh?"

She shook her head to dislodge his finger. "I didn't lie to you, Evan. Josh and I are—were—good friends after you left. We both missed you, and there was a moment when we could have been more to each other. But we…we never crossed that line. And since I started taking care of him, he flirts and I banter. That's it."

"You find him attractive, though." It wasn't a question.

She shrugged and looked at Evan's chest. "Sure. A woman would have to be blind not to think so. He has good genes, like his brother."

She could have lied and said no, but he'd have read straight through her and that would put an end to any hope she had to… What? *Make him love you again?*

No, no, no, that hadn't been the plan. A few yummy orgasms. That was the plan.

Not anymore.

Swallowing back the implications of her new reality, she looked up to see if he'd caught any of the emotions filtering over her face, but he seemed lost in his own thoughts.

He nodded absently, and some of the tension eased from his body. He met her gaze again and grazed the backs of his fingers over her cheek. "I'm sorry. I forgot for a minute that you're not a trained submissive and Josh isn't a Dom. He doesn't know the rules. He doesn't understand the boundaries not to cross with another Dom's sub. When I saw him ogling your tits, I saw red."

"You think of me as your sub?" *Is that all I'll ever be, or will it lead to more?*

He was quiet for a moment, his blue eyes taking on a hollow, haunted look, as if he'd gone to some faraway place. His silence hurt. Was it really that hard to think of her that way? *Aren't I enough?*

You weren't nine years ago.

His jaw ticked, and his eyes cleared, focusing on her with lust and a hardness that made her shiver. "Yes, I do. So I'll make one more thing clear before we move forward, like I did for Josh just now. While you and I are together, until our time here is over, you are mine. You might work for Josh, but you are mine. Do you understand?"

Shayna still wasn't sure if his jealousy was just the Dom thing or if Evan had feelings for her, but she was ready to admit, if only to herself, she *was* his, always had been. Realizing she'd never truly stopped loving him should have scared her shitless, especially when he kept saying "right now" and had just added "until our time here is over." It didn't bode well for her heart.

"Shayna?" he prompted, his fingers on her arms tightening in a deliciously bruising grip that washed reason from her brain. But the ache in her tummy competed with the pleasure.

Right now, until it was over, forever—it made no difference. She could only go by what she saw in his eyes. *Right now,* he wanted *her*. *Right now, she* was the only woman his body burned for. That was enough...for right now. It would have to be.

She strained against his arms, relishing the pain her efforts caused, and rubbed her aching nipples against his chest to drive out the self-preservation lurking behind her need. "Yes, Evan. I understand completely. I'm yours to do with as you want."

Until you don't.

His fingers relaxed, then released her only to find the hem of her shirt. "Arms up."

Her biceps screamed as she raised her arms for him to pull the T-shirt over her head. He tossed it aside, then palmed her breasts and squeezed. Pain slashed from her nipples to her pussy, and heat pooled in her clit. She closed her eyes and moaned.

"You have no idea how much I want to make you come."

She blinked her eyes open. "I won't stop you."

A smile tugged at his lips and erased the frown lines from his forehead. His icy eyes melted to the color of a blue flame. "No, you won't. But I'm not through punishing you."

Another shiver ran through her, and in that moment, she silently relinquished her body and will to Evan, trusting him to know exactly what she needed. "Am I going to like this punishment?"

"I hope so." He lowered his head until his lips brushed hers. His nimble fingers unzipped her skirt, and it floated over her hips to her feet. He stood back and looked at her. "I know I will."

He crossed to his black duffel in the corner and pulled out the wrist cuffs she'd worn that afternoon. "Turn around and put your hands behind your back."

Spinning to face the desk, she thrust her wrists together at the base of her spine. The stretch of her nipples brought another moan as the sting of the clamps spread across her breasts like a thousand needles.

As soon as her wrists were secured with the cuffs, something plopped on the floor behind her. He turned her to face him again. "On your knees."

Mustering as much grace as possible, she lowered to her knees and sat back on her heels. She grimaced, once again aware of the butt plug and the warm tingling around her sphincter. Not that she'd forgotten it was there. Accustomed to it was a better description.

He shrugged out of his shirt, revealing those washboard abs she'd promised herself to explore. She wasn't sure she'd be able to keep that promise since he was determined to keep her hog-tied. The button of his jeans gave way, and he dragged the zipper down. His thumbs hooked the waist and shoved the dark denim down his hips. His hard, thick erection bowed toward his belly button, and her mouth filled with saliva as she realized his intent. She licked her lips to wet them.

He stepped closer, one hand fisted around his shaft. The other palmed the side of her face, his thumb tracing her lower lip. "I'm going to fuck your sweet mouth now. Are you ready?"

Nodding, she raised on her knees. Her tongue glided over her lips again and licked his thumb. He groaned and reached behind her head to twist her ponytail around his hand until her scalp stung. As the broad head touched her lips, she laved around the ridge, then closed her mouth over the crown.

His hips jerked, shoving his cock to the back of her throat. Without hesitation, she sucked in her cheeks and swirled her tongue around the velvety shaft, the way she remembered he liked it.

His head fell back. "Oh yeah, that's it."

Her breathing turned shallow as he slowly pumped in and out. She tried to take him deeper and groaned her frustration when he held her in place. Between the sting of her scalp and the pleasure on his face, her body was humming. She wriggled her hips to create fiction on her clit. If she could reach it, she'd be off to the races.

"You're enjoying this punishment far too much."

He pulled out of her mouth, ignoring her cry of disappointment, and dragged her to her feet. He kicked the pillow out of his way and spun her around to face the end of the desk. Gripping her elbows, he guided her until the top of her thighs hit the edge.

His hips ground against her ass, mashing his hard, hot erection into her crack. He inhaled sharply. "You don't have a clue what you do to me. You keep me at the end of my rope, barely hanging on to my control."

She blew out a breath to get a loose strand of hair out of her eyes and partly to release her exasperation. "When will you understand, Evan? I don't want you to hold back. I want you to lose control, like you did that night."

He growled, and before she could blink, he swept a hand over his desk, sending the things on his desk crashing to the floor. He was always neat and orderly, to the point of compulsion. His disregard for his workspace because of her made her smile, and her pussy contracted. Juices trickled down her thighs.

The pressure at her elbows tipped her forward until her chest met the cold desktop. She laid her cheek against it, facing the door. It was open, but she couldn't spare an ounce of concern.

He tapped the end of the butt plug, and his breath tickled her ear. "You will not come until I give you permission, or you'll be wearing that thing all day tomorrow. Is that clear?"

She bit her lip to keep from telling him she wasn't far from disobeying and nodded.

One booted foot shoved her feet apart, and he squatted behind her. "Just as I thought. Dripping wet."

As his tongue dipped into her passage, Shayna squealed and arched off the desk. The rough pad flattened against her throbbing clit and swiped up to the flange of the plug. Her moan reverberated through the room, and she lifted her ass for more. He gave it to her in the form of two fingers. She tried to buck against them to drive them deeper, but his other hand griped her ass to keep her still.

"Mmm, nice and tight." He scissored his fingers a few times, then withdrew. "Tastes good, just like I remember." He stood and bent over her, his mouth grazing the curve of her shoulder. "Don't move."

Closing her eyes, she heard the tear of a wrapper and held her breath in anticipation. The heat of his body and the rough denim against her legs was her only warning before he crammed her full of his cock in one hard thrust. The plug made the fit tighter. She squirmed to adjust to the fullness, but there was no give.

She craned her head back, arching her back for better depth. "Oh my god, Evan. I... It...mmmmmm."

"Fuck, yes."

And then he took on the same leisurely outward drag as he had that afternoon but this time he had to screw his way in. Heat blasted her core. Her fingers clutched at air. His dug into her hips, setting off tiny sparks of pleasure.

"Please let me come." She was so close. She wasn't sure she could perch on the edge much longer.

He ignored her plea, and the next thrust came too shallow to hit her G-spot, giving her a slight reprieve yet making her want to cry. She concentrated on her breathing, which seemed to help some. That and relaxing her core muscles. The tighter she squeezed, the closer she came to the peak.

Bending over her, his chest pressed her into the unrelenting maple desk, crushing her arms between them. The strain only added to the fire building inside her.

"He wants you," he whispered. "He wants to fuck your pretty pussy, but it's mine."

Did he mean Josh? That didn't make sense. Only five minutes ago, he'd thrown a hissy fit about his brother. Why would he bring him up in the middle of—

"Open your eyes, Shay." He nuzzled her temple. "See the lust in his eyes as he watches me fuck you."

Chapter Nine

Blinking, Shayna slowly lifted her eyelids. She couldn't have heard Evan right. But there Josh stood, filling the doorway. His blue eyes, like Evan's, glistened with lust and focused squarely on where their bodies joined. His hand cupped his crotch, adjusting the obvious erection beneath the denim.

Her gaze flew to his face. The inner muscles of her sex clenched as the memory of Evan's expression when he'd watched her nine years ago with Tucker superimposed over Josh's.

"You like that, don't you, Shay? Having someone watch?" Evan's voice was rough, and thick like strong bourbon.

"You," she said, her words in time with the plunge of his cock. "Having…you…watch."

He growled and turned his head to look at Josh. "Get out."

Josh's eyes locked with hers, silently asking if she was okay, if she wanted him to intervene.

In answer, she closed her eyes and tilted her pussy into Evan's next thrust. She didn't have to look to know they were alone again. Her brain tried to intrude, tried to analyze Evan's actions, his words, his motives, but the head of his cock hit the sensitive bundle of nerves on her inner wall, and she shut the door on anything but the sound of her blood rushing though her ears and trying to hold off the mother of all orgasms.

Because that's what Evan wanted, and something deep inside her, something that had nothing to do with her love for him, needed to give him what he wanted. Was that what it meant to be a submissive?

He kissed her shoulder, his breath rushing over her skin, and stilled. "Good girl."

Good girl? Had she passed some test? Was her punishment over? Would she now get her reward? She sighed. "Can I come now?"

"No." He straightened and abruptly pulled out. The sound of his zipper was like a splash of icy water to her brain. "Your punishment is complete."

"But—" Her core still hummed, and she yearned for an orgasm. They couldn't be done. "But you said I couldn't come until you gave me permission."

"That's right." He uncuffed her wrists and rubbed the circulation back into her arms. "And you obeyed perfectly."

His meaning took hold, and her mouth hung

open. What the fuck? She swung her head to glare at him over her shoulder. "You weren't going to give me permission, were you?"

"No." He held her down with one hand when she tried to rise. "Maybe the next time I tell you not to come, you'll think twice. And maybe next time, I'll give you so many orgasms you'll be begging me to stop…but I won't."

She shivered at the hedonistic promise. Was that possible? To have so many orgasms that she'd beg for relief?

I don't think so.

She smiled. He was welcome to try.

His fingers gripped the plug's base. "Breathe out and push."

Propping her upper body on her elbows, she did as instructed, and he tugged. As the plug's widest girth stretched her sphincter, a euphoric burn had her moaning. Then it was gone, and she felt so empty.

He chuckled. "You definitely need your ass fucked."

If that was what it felt like, then yes, she most certainly did. "When?"

"Not tonight." He handed her skirt and T-shirt to her but pulled her into his arms and lowered his lips to brush hers. "Go on up to bed."

His thick erection behind his jeans prodded

her belly, leaving her hopeful. "Yours?"

He shook his head and set her back. "Yours."

"But—"

"No buts." He took her shirt from her and held it up. "You need to get dressed before your body temp drops and you get cold."

"Because of the adrenaline?"

His gaze snapped to hers. "How did you know that?"

"I'm a nurse, remember." She smiled and stuck her arms into the T-shirt. "I know things."

"Is that so?" He tugged it down her arms. "Well, Miss Know It All, get your sweet ass upstairs like I told you. I'll be up there in a minute to take care of you."

She poked her head through the neck hole. "Does that mean orgasms?"

"It means a spanking if you don't obey." He turned to collect the plug and condom wrapper. "We still need to get those clamps off."

Stepping into the skirt and zipping it, she hesitated. "Evan?"

"Yeah?" He stuffed the cuffs back in his bag, and she suddenly wondered how many other women had worn them and if they were cleaned between each use.

She couldn't think of that right now but knew the nurse in her would demand she eventually bring up the topic. "I need to, um, check on—"

He looked up at her from where he squatted. "I'll see to Josh tonight."

Nodding, she slipped into her flip-flops and stepped toward him. "Evan?"

He straightened and lifted a hand to brush the back of his fingers over her cheek. "Are you angling for another punishment?"

Placing her hands on his chest, she looked up at him from under her lashes. "I only wanted to say thank you…for my punishment."

The corners of his lips turned up, and his eyes softened. "You are most welcome."

With that, she turned on her heel and walked out of the room, adding a little extra sway to her hips. She might still be aching for release, but she'd never felt this free in her life. And if the look on his face told her anything, it was that she'd broken through one more wall surrounding his heart and taken away one more excuse to rebuild it.

****

As Shayna swaggered from his office, another notch in the rope around Evan's chest loosened.

Never in a million years—or at any time in the last nine—would he have imagined her in the role of a sub. He'd thought her beyond his reach and rightfully so with his distorted memory of that night. But this afternoon and tonight, he'd begun to wonder if they could make it work, if she was the reason he'd never had a relationship with any of his subs. And not because of the guilt, but because he'd never stopped loving her.

He dared not get his hopes up yet that she would love him back or that she'd even be able to accept him. There were still many things about him she didn't know or might never understand, might not be able to live with.

And yet she'd been so fucking beautiful kneeling before him, looking at him with adoration and eagerly awaiting her punishment like a good little sub. She'd taken her punishment with relish and thanked him without prompt. And she'd finally put him first, before Josh. She'd also made Evan realize she might actually be able to fit into his world.

Until he knew for sure…

Putting aside a wish that might never come true, he disposed of the condom, cleaned the plug, and put it back in its case. Grabbing his bag, he headed to the front room to check on Josh.

Evan found him already in bed, watching a baseball game. "Do you need anything before I head upstairs?"

Josh's gaze cut from the television to level Evan with a hard stare. "Is Shayna okay?"

"She's fine." He struggled to keep from smiling as the vision of her ass swishing out of the office filled his mind. His brother didn't understand and wouldn't appreciate his pleasure.

As if to affirm Evan's thoughts, Josh shook his head. "Why does she need that?"

Setting the bag at his feet, he leaned against the doorframe and crossed his arms over his chest. "I can't speak for her, and I wouldn't tell you if I knew. You're free to ask her in the morning."

Josh's lips thinned and a frown wrinkled his forehead. "Why do *you* need it?"

He hadn't seen that one coming. "You've never asked me that. Why now?"

That got him a shrug. "I figured you'd tell me if you wanted me to know, but after…" He waved a hand in the direction of the office on the other side of the stairs.

Evan straightened. "Honestly, Josh, I don't know. Sometimes these needs stem from something in a person's past, something traumatic, but I don't have anything like that to make me want this way of life. I just do."

Josh grew quiet, then he nodded.

Knowing he should let the subject drop but unable to stop the words from pouring out of his mouth, he asked, "It excited you, didn't it? What you saw tonight."

"Fuck, Ev, you know it did. I don't think there's a man alive who wouldn't have spiked a boner. It was better than porn." He blew out a breath. "Not the bondage part, though. I can do without that."

Evan smiled, feeling the tension between them dissolve even as the thought of Shayna being the target of his brother's horny thoughts rankled. "Fair enough."

His feet itching to get to her, he let the conversation go. "Night."

"Night."

Evan turned away and headed to the kitchen to grab a couple of bottles of water, then took the stairs two at a time, his step lighter than it had been in months. Josh had finally talked to him about his choices without judging, maybe even understanding him a little more. And the woman he'd loved for more years than he cared to count had accepted him and everything that came with him.

Well, not everything, but he wouldn't think about that right now.

After stopping by the bathroom to collect a couple of towels and a warm, wet washcloth, he walked through Shayna's door. She wasn't on the bed, and it took him a minute to scan the room to find her. She stood by the window, staring out into the inky darkness, still dressed except for the flip-flops. She'd taken her hair down and was brushing it in long, slow strokes.

He wanted to join her, to wrap his arms

around her and simply hold her. Instead, he shut the door softly, lowered the bag to the floor, and sat on the end of the bed. He'd already taken too long with Josh. "Come here, darlin'. Let me take care of you."

Startled, she spun around. "I didn't hear you come in."

"You should be resting." He crooked a finger at her.

She hesitated, only for a second, then closed the distance between them. He spread his legs and pulled her closer. Unzipping her skirt, he let it drop, then removed her shirt. Her breasts bounced then lifted as she clasped her hands behind her back without instruction. His mouth watered, and the rope around his chest uncoiled a little more. He gently palmed them, weighing them. He licked one, then the other.

"Mmmmmm" Her head fell back, her lips parting.

Part of him wanted to give her the relief she craved, but that would defeat the purpose of tonight's scene. "I'm going to remove the clamps. It's going to hurt."

"Good."

His cock jerked, straining for freedom from the confines of his jeans. Jesus, she was going to kill him. "I'm going to help ease some of that pain, and judging from your reactions to it so far, you could experience a need to come, but you are not to do so."

"Mmm."

"Shayna?"

"I understand. No orgasms," she muttered, her frustration evident.

Chuckling, he unscrewed the tiny vise on the right breast and watched the little red bud plump up as he removed it.

"Freakin' hell." She bit her lip and squeezed her eyes shut tight.

Evan covered her nipple with his mouth and sucked, laving the taut tip with the flat of his tongue, mashing it to the roof of his mouth. He watched her breathe through the pleasure-pain, then released her and repeated the process on the opposite breast.

Squeezing the pale globes together, he kissed each one. "I'm proud of you, Shay. You've done well. I'm very pleased."

Her eyes blinked open, moisture glistening in them, but the sparkle in them and her preening posture told him she was happy with the praise.

A rush of emotion rose inside him, but he tamped it down. Before he let himself fully embrace a possible future with her, he had to be sure she'd accept everything about him and his lifestyle. They weren't quite there yet.

He stood and handed her a bottle of water. "Drink. You need to hydrate."

Downing his in several long pulls, he waited for her to drink at least half the bottle, then motioned to the bed. "Lie down on your stomach."

Looking at the cloth in his hand, she bit her bottom lip. "I already washed up. Was I not supposed to?"

"That's my job. I need to make sure you're okay." He tossed the cloth on the rug at his feet. "Next time, let me do it."

"Understood, but really, I'm more than okay." She crawled up the bed and flopped down at the center of the mattress. "Can I ask you a question? Well, several questions."

"Of course."

"Good, 'cause I have a million."

"Move your hair."

Gathering her thick mane, she balled it into a knot at the top of her head, then placed her arms outward, fingers toward the side of the bed, and faced him.

"Ask away." He retrieved a jar of shea butter from his bag and scooted onto the bed beside her hip. To keep the chill off, he pulled the sheet up to her waist, then slathered his hands with the lotion and rubbed it into the back, arm, and shoulder.

"First things first." Her brows furrowed and her lips thinned. "Is your equipment clean?"

Grinning, he glanced down at his dick prodding against his jeans. "Um, I'm pretty sure I took a shower earlier."

She rolled her eyes. "You know what I mean. I can't do these tie-me-up contraptions and anal toys with you anymore unless I know they haven't been used on another sub and that you're cleaning them after use. I have sanitary issues."

He heard the nurse in her and respected her *issues*. He felt the same. "Believe me, I take cleanliness very seriously. If it makes you feel better, everything in that bag is new. All bought before coming here."

"Okay, because that was starting to freak me out."

He nodded and began to massage the cream into her right buttocks where bruises dotted her pale skin and more would no doubt show up by morning.

Obviously satisfied, she closed her eyes and relaxed into his ministrations, only an occasional twinge marring her face when he hit a sore spot.

"Why'd you wait?" Her voice was soft, almost inaudible. "Why didn't you want to have sex with me?"

He pressed his thumbs into her upper thigh. "I'd ask for more information, but I can tell you honestly, there has never been a time since I've known you that I didn't want to have sex with you."

A blush spread over her lovely cheeks, and she opened her eyes. "That's not what I meant. Back when we were together, that summer, why'd it take pushing you to your limits to get you to have sex with me? I was ready by our third date."

How did he explain that, by their third date, he'd had an overwhelming need to fuck her hard and fast? He'd fantasized about it. But she was so sweet and he'd wanted her first time to be gentle and slow. "You have no idea how bad I wanted to. So bad it hurt. But you were a virgin, and I was afraid to hurt you. You kept me at the end of a tether, all lathered up every minute of the day and night. You were like a drug, and I felt out of control."

A sadness filled her eyes. "And I was scared to tell you how much I needed you. You were always so intense, and I just wanted to shake all that tension out of you, for you to let go."

He caught the tear that dripped from one corner of her eye. "We were a pair, huh?" When she didn't say anything, he said, "But I couldn't have been what you needed back then. I had to work through my shit."

"I suppose."

The past was unchangeable. He could only

control the present.

Placing the sheet higher to cover what he'd massaged, he moved down the mattress and uncovered her leg. Starting with her upper thigh, he worked his way down its silky smoothness.

While he worked, he tried to lighten the mood. "What else is spinning in that beautiful, naughty head of yours?"

A smile pulled at one corner of her mouth. "Well…" She bit her lip again and looked at the headboard, as if running through a long list for the right question. "You said you still like to watch and you do it at your club. I guess you've had a lot of submissives."

Both statements sounded more like questions, and though there'd never been anyone special, he didn't want to talk to Shayna about his past partners. "Do *you* want to tell *me* about your past sexual partners?"

She lifted a brow, and he was reminded she already had.

"Okay, I'll tell you this. I've never slept with a sub." He lifted her foot and rubbed the arch, and she moaned. "Except for the last one, I've never had a relationship with any of them and we always met at the club. Never in a personal space. And when the scene was done, we went our separate ways."

Her muscles tightened. "The last one?"

Out of all that, she'd gotten stuck on that bit of truth.

"It's hard to explain." Evan stopped to look at her over the tips of her toes. "Clay is the Dom I've partnered with over the last few years. We like the same things, and we used to take turns being in charge."

He went back to his task, rubbing her toes. "About six months ago, he met a woman outside the club and fell ass over heels in love. He wanted to make sure she could fit into the lifestyle, so I was invited to join them as their third. He and Lindsey have been inseparable ever since. They're actually engaged now, and I've been meaning to find a new partner, which is why I bought new equipment."

"Why did you want a new partner?"

"Because Clay won't give up the lead, and I wouldn't either, were I him. Lindsey is his woman. But I need more. I need to take charge of a scene. I can't always be second in command, so to speak. Does that make sense?

"Yes, but why have you waited this long to find a new Dom to work with? Is she special to you?" Her words were tinged with jealousy, making him smile.

To hide his amusement, he kissed her toes and shifted to her other side to work his way back up "Do you want some more water?"

"No." She looked at him expectantly.

She wasn't giving up, and he had nothing to hide. "She's special, but not in the way you think. I think you'd really like her. But to answer you more clearly, she is a good friend."

Like Josh is to you.

Somehow that didn't sit well at the bottom of his gut, he welcomed the silence when it settled over the room.

He moved up her leg, savoring the silky texture. He could spend all night touching her, relearning every curve, every hidden treasure. She'd changed. The slight build of her youth had blossomed, her hips flaring more, her stomach and legs more toned. Her breasts were fuller, and her mound was neatly manicured. He loved it all.

"Would you want to watch me with another man?"

His cock, only semi-erect from having given up on plowing into her vise-like pussy, jerked back to life. Images of her with Tucker filled his mind. Would he like to watch her with another man? That was like asking if he needed to breathe.

Before he could answer, she rushed on. "Or would you prefer a second woman? Have you ever done that? I know it's a big turn on for a man, two women having sex."

He tucked the sheet around her leg and moved up the bed to start on her left ass cheek and lower back. "Is that something you want to try?"

"Not really." Her gaze flew to his. "But I would do it…if that's what you want."

He chuckled at her frankness and her eagerness to please. "I'm not opposed to that scenario. Voyeurism for me has more to do with the pleasure you receive. However, I do prefer a straight scene."

"Why? I mean, my confidence wouldn't survive watching you with another woman." Another rosy flush tinted her face. She'd obviously shared more than she meant to. "But what do you get from it? A jealousy high? Some kind of cuckhold thing?"

"No, jealousy has nothing to do with it." Not really. Maybe a little. But he would love to see the expression on her face as another man gave her pleasure. And seeing her pussy swallow another cock… Fucking hot. "It's more about the visual."

"Yes, men and their visual stimulation."

He finished her upper body and put the jar on the side table. "Turn on your side, facing the door."

Fitting himself against her back, on top of the sheet, he rained kisses on her shoulder, neck, and ear. "You can mock visual stimulation, but you have to admit, you liked knowing I was watching you with Tucker. I saw it in your eyes. It made you feel powerful because you knew how turned-on I was."

"Yes." She yawned. "But mostly it was that *I* was the one making you hot."

No doubt about that. He placed an arm over her waist and rested his chin on the top of her head. He'd wait until she fell asleep to go take another cold shower.

She turned her head to glance over her shoulder. "Were you turned on tonight? When Josh came in?"

If he thought past his jealousy, there could only be one answer. "Yes."

Shayna wiggled her ass against his groin. "And you're still turned on."

"Yes."

"I could take care of that for you."

Lust swept through him like a Texas wildfire, and for a moment, he nearly accepted her invitation. "Normally, I would have fucked your mouth, your pussy, and your ass and come several times during your punishment, all while keeping you close but not close enough to climax. But you're not trained and I can't expect total obedience."

She turned completely on her back to peer up at him with wide eyes. "So you're punishing yourself, too?"

Yeah, he was a twisted motherfucker. "I am."

Her eyes glistened with moisture. "I'm sorry. I promise to try harder because it breaks my heart for you to suffer."

He rolled to his back and barked out a laugh. She shoved at his shoulder, and he hauled her against his chest. "Darlin', this is the best kind of suffering I've ever known."

With a snort, she settled, and it wasn't long before her breathing evened out. He closed his eyes. Only a few more minutes, and he'd get up. If he was going to suffer, he wanted to do it while he was holding her rather than in a cold bed alone.

Just for a little while, anyway.

Chapter Ten

In the early light of dawn, Evan woke to the sound of a quiet murmur and the warmth of soft feminine curves nestled against him. For a moment, his sleep-fogged brain panicked, grasping for an explanation of who she was and how she came to be in his bed. He hadn't slept with a woman since…ever.

Then her vanilla scent registered, and a different panic took hold. Shayna. He hadn't meant to fall asleep, hadn't meant to draw from the comfort of her presence next to him, hadn't meant to have the best sleep of his life.

His morning wood had him grinding his hips into her backside before he caught himself. He wanted to wake her up and make love to her. Take his time, kiss her awake, slide deep into her heat, and whisper words of love.

But he couldn't. Not yet. He had to be certain she could accept one more aspect of who he was, because making love to Shayna would be a commitment he couldn't take back.

Easing from the bed, he tried not to wake her. He'd cook breakfast for Josh and let her sleep in.

She'd start her weekend shift tomorrow night, and he didn't want her starting out dead on her feet.

In his room, he changed out of his jeans into a clean pair and donned a fresh T-shirt. Grabbing his boots and socks, he snuck past her door and headed downstairs.

Josh hobbled out of the front room on his crutch as Evan sat on the bottom steps to put on his socks and shove his feet into his boots. He stood and turned toward the kitchen. "Give me a sec, and I'll make us something to eat."

"You do remember that Doc Callahan's coming out today?" Josh asked.

"Yep."

"He'll do an ultrasound to see if Star's ready." Josh followed him. "I think she is. At least, I hope so or—" His phone rang. He glanced at the screen and turned away. "Hello."

Evan gathered eggs, butter, bacon, and biscuits from the fridge and started cooking breakfast, the only thing he knew how to make. He understood Josh's concerns. They'd invested a lot of money in the new mare, and breeding horses was his brother's dream.

"Fuck, we're going to miss our window." Josh had hung up from his call and was scrolling through his phone one-handed. "Doc's wife had a car wreck. Just a fender bender, but he's taking her to the hospital. He can't be here 'til next week."

"I'm sure we can find another vet," Evan said, turning the bacon. His stomach growled. He'd skipped supper last night, and the sandwiches from lunch by the lake yesterday hadn't been much. Damn, was that just yesterday?

Josh lowered himself to a chair. "I can try."

Thirty minutes later, Evan got up from the table, having crammed five pieces of bacon, three eggs, and four biscuits down his throat. There wouldn't be time for lunch.

He cleaned his plate and set aside something for Shayna's breakfast.

"Damn." Josh laid his phone down and bit into a biscuit, butter smearing across his mouth. If Shayna saw the amount of grease they'd consumed, she'd be the one having the coronary.

"No luck?" He grabbed a bottle of water from the fridge.

Shaking his head, Josh looked up at Evan. "Don't you have a friend who's a rancher? Can he recommend someone?"

"I'll give him a call." Thinking of Clay brought Evan back to his plan for Shayna and figuring out how to execute it. He could take her to Silver House. Tate would be willing to be their third if he was available. But the dungeon and a stranger might be too much for her first ménage.

"Like now, Ev," Josh prodded, interrupting his strategies.

Mentally rolling his eyes, Evan pulled out his phone and scrolled through his contacts for Clay's number. Bradi Kincaid caught his eye before he got to the C's, and he stopped. She was an intern at a veterinarian clinic specializing in large animals. "Hang on. I might not have to call Clay."

He pressed the call button and listened to it ring. He hadn't known Bradi long, but he figured she owed him one since he'd been instrumental in pushing Mason Montgomery into acting on his feelings for her. They were now engaged to be married.

"Bradi Kincaid," the voice on the other end of the line said.

"Hey, Bradi, it's Evan. Do you have a minute? I need your help."

"Anything for you, Ev."

"Don't let Mason hear you say that. *Anything* could get really interesting."

"So I understand, but you're right. Mason doesn't share." She sounded winded, as if she'd run a mile. "What can I do for you?"

"I wondered if you'd be free around noon and wouldn't mind driving over to Stone Creek to help me out. The vet we had coming to inseminate can't make it, and we can't find anyone else. We don't want to miss the window. Is this something you can do?"

"I've done more than a dozen this month—all

moms-to-be are doing well—but give me a minute to check with Doc Harper." He heard some rustling and then voices.

"What did he say?" Josh asked.

"*She* has to—"

"Doc says he can spare me," Bradi said. "I can be there around eleven thirty. Is that okay?"

"Perfect."

"Text me the address."

"Will do. See you then." He hung up.

Josh sat up a little straighter. "She'll do it?"

Evan tucked his cell in his back pocket and headed to the back door. "Be here before noon."

"Wait, is she a real doctor?"

"Yes."

His eyes narrowed. "She one of your playthings?"

Evan reached for his hat, settled it on his head, and turned to Josh. "Not that it's any of your business, but no, she's just a friend. And she's engaged, so keep your good hand to yourself or Mason will break it *and* your other leg."

"I was thinking of Shayna," his brother grumbled around a mouthful of egg. "Besides, I have enough to occupy my good hand right now."

Evan thought about the stable of women who'd visited Monday morning before Shayna arrived, but then it dawned on him that they hadn't been around since. He had to wonder if it was a coincidence or if Josh was hiding them from her.

Soured by the notion, he let the back door slam a little harder on his way out, then immediately regretted it. He hoped he hadn't woken Shayna.

Fuck, it was going to be a long day.

****

The house was quiet when Shayna finally made it downstairs, her muscles resisting each step in a way that made her feel free and sexy…and happy. Which wouldn't last long if this slow burn between her and Evan went up in flames.

Entering the kitchen, she went straight to the note on the table. The scrawled handwriting was Josh's, and there wasn't much of it.

If the vet comes to the house looking for me, I'm at the barn.

Hmph. If he was able to get down to the barn on his own, he was feeling well enough not to need her. She'd become more of his housekeeper than nurse in the last couple of weeks, and she suspected the sneaky devil played helpless to keep her here because he thought she and Evan would work things out. That, and he liked those sponge baths. Maybe a little too much. She'd have to tell him her time here was coming to an end and then look for another weekday position.

But that meant leaving Evan, too. Which was probably for the best. The longer she stayed, the deeper she'd fall and the more painful it would be when he grew bored with her and moved on.

With a sigh, she began prepping for lunch. Besides not wanting to wait until evening to see Evan, to gauge where she stood with him after last night, she wanted to surprise the others with lunch in celebration of Josh's big day, the first insemination on his horse farm. But she'd have to make something light and easy for the guys to eat quickly. Josh wouldn't want to take time out for a big meal.

By eleven fifteen, she had sandwiches packed and a bag filled with assorted fruit and oatmeal raisin bars she'd made. They'd never know she'd used soy instead of flour.

Just as she was about to head out the back door, the crunch of gravel on the front drive signaled the arrival of the vet. She opened the screen door and stepped out onto the front porch as a four-door pickup pulled up.

The ponytailed brunette getting out of the driver's side didn't look like Doc Callahan, though. She wore snug jeans that clung to her long slender legs, a red sleeveless shirt that showed off tanned sculpted arms, and boots that had seen better days.

The passenger door opened, and a similarly built blonde slid out. That's where the similarities ended. This one was all bangles and beads with her short skirt and flirty pink blouse that revealed more cleavage than it covered. Matching pointed-toed pink boots completed her ensemble, and her long wavy hair blew in the breeze like a model in a shampoo commercial.

No doubt, more of Josh's women, though they'd never come in twos. Somehow, Shayna didn't question his ability to manage both, even without the use of an arm and a leg.

The brunette trotted up the porch steps and held out her hand. "Dr. Bradi Kincaid. Evan is expecting me."

It took Shayna a few seconds to process her words. She certainly didn't look like any vet Shayna had ever known, but she thrust out her hand to shake the other woman's. "Sorry, I was expecting Doc Callahan."

"Oh, was he able to get here after all?" Bradi asked, stepping aside as the blonde climbed the last step.

Shayna shrugged. "I don't know. I guess I'm out of the loop on this one."

"That's okay," the blonde said. "We'll just have a visit with Evan."

Jealousy streaked through Shayna, but she ignored it and held out her hand. "I'm Shayna."

The woman clasped her hand with a delicate, manicured grip. "Lindsey."

Lindsey? The *Lindsey?* Air stalled in Shayna's lungs, and her heart took a tumble. *Here?*

She let go of Lindsey's hand and tried to breathe. Evan had had sex with this woman, and from their talk last night, clearly, she was special to him. Shayna couldn't think past that.

Blue eyes darted to Bradi in question, then back at Shayna. "Is Ev here?"

What was she doing *here*? Shayna understood why the lady vet was here, but what was this one here for? To play nurse?

Shayna mentally snorted. She'd thought that role was hers. "He's down at the barn."

Lindsey smiled, perfect white teeth around perfect pink lips. Lips that had been on Evan's body, doing things that gave him pleasure. "Do you mind if we use the restroom before Bradi does her thing? It's been a long drive."

In a trance, Shayna nodded and opened the screen door. "The door past the stairs."

Bradi went first, leaving Shayna alone with Lindsey. No, she couldn't do this.

"If you'll excuse me, I was just about to take lunch down to the guys?" She started in the direction of the kitchen. "I'd better get to it."

Lindsey followed her. "I've always wondered

what Evan's family home looked like. He's pretty closed lip about personal stuff."

What could be more personal than fucking?

Shayna gathered water bottles in a plastic sack, trying not to vomit those words. Trying not to vomit, period. Her stomach twisted and rolled, threatening to heave. She needed air. She needed to be anywhere but here in her ratty jean shorts and faded T-shirt.

She busied herself, putting away condiments, replacing a roll of paper towels, anything to prevent having to look at the beautiful woman in Evan's life, his intimate life. Images of them in various acts, those he'd done to Shayna, those they'd talked about last night, flicked through her brain like erotic silent movies.

"Are you Josh's girlfriend?" the woman asked.

Why would she think that? And why wouldn't she just shut up?

"No, just the hired nurse." *Nobody special.*

Bradi poked her head through the door. "It's all yours."

Lindsey swaggered out of the kitchen—thank god—and Shayna drew in a searing breath. The back of her eyelids burned, so she scrubbed the counters and kept her back to Bradi. Had she slept with Evan, too? Probably. She was as beautiful as Lindsey.

Bradi's cell rang, and she answered quickly.

"Yes, I know, Mason, but we just got here, and I had to pee." She laughed. "I will tell Evan you said so."

Shayna blinked at the ceiling, but the damn tear spilled anyway. Why had she let down her guard and lost her heart to a man who had beautiful vets and supermodels in his life?

What the hell am I doing here? I should just get in my car and go home, clean my apartment, see my mom, rescue a dog, anything but stay here and torture myself.

"I'll let you know when we head home," Bradi said. "I love you, too. Bye." To Shayna, she said, "I swear the man thinks I'm helpless. I've probably changed more flats than he has."

"Oh, let him do his man thing." Lindsey was back, hanging her arm across Bradi's shoulders. "You know you love it."

Cheeks flushed, Bradi grinned. "I really do."

So maybe the vet wasn't involved with Evan in a personal way. Thank god for small favors.

"Which way to the barn?" Bradi asked. "My equipment is in the truck. I'll have to drive."

"It's just around back a bit." Shayna thrust a thumb over her shoulder.

Lindsey unwound herself from Bradi. "We'll give you a lift, so you don't have to carry all this."

Panic shot through Shayna. She didn't want to be anywhere near these two for longer than necessary. In fact, surprising Evan with lunch no longer held the same appeal, and she paled miserably in comparison to the surprise in his kitchen. "No, that's okay. I can manage."

"I insist." Lindsey grabbed the basket from the table and followed Bradi out the front door.

Glaring at the woman's back, Shayna snatched up the bag of fruit, bars, and waters and joined the two women at the truck. She tossed the sacks on top of the basket, not caring one whit that she'd smushed the sandwiches.

"I'll just sit back here," she said, pointing to the tailgate, "to make sure nothing falls over."

"Oh, fun." Lindsey's smile was genuine and somewhat disarming as she plopped her perfect heart-shaped ass on the gate beside Shayna. "I haven't done this since I was a teenager."

Bradi aimed the truck toward the back of the house, and they rocked along on the road to the barn.

"Have you known Evan and Josh long?" The girl was a talker. That was certain.

"I haven't seen them in nine years until recently, but we all grew up here." Shayna stared at the clouds of dirt billowing around her flip-flopped feet, then at the pink boots dangling beside them. She should have worn something nicer to surprise Evan. Now she'd be a weed amongst roses. A weed wearing flip-flops.

The truck stopped, and Shayna jumped off the tailgate. She snatched up the basket just as Evan sauntered out of the barn. Her stomach flipped and churned all at the same time. Josh appeared, leaning his good shoulder against the doorframe. Mark stood beside him, gawking at the women the same way he'd stared at her over the past weeks. Now she wasn't a weed. She was chopped liver.

Lindsey passed Shayna in a rush and collided with Evan's chest in an embrace that sliced through her like broken glass.

"Hey, what are you doing here?" His startled gaze darted from Lindsey's face to Shayna.

Looking away from his hands on the woman's shoulders, not wishing to see if he returned the hug, she focused on Josh as she skirted the couple and kept going through the barn to the other side.

She set the basket on a covered barrel, then motioned to Cal and Rusty under the only shade by the back paddock. "Anyone hungry?"

They strolled over, and she stepped back to let them choose. The sooner the basket was empty, the sooner she could get back to the house and get the hell out of here.

She had no right to be jealous. She didn't own him. They weren't exclusive. She was just using him for orgasms, and he was teaching her how to get what she wanted safely. *Right?*

"I'll take bologna if you have one," Josh said

behind her.

Yeah, that's what it sounds like. Utter bologna.

"Sure." She forced a smile and turned to hand him the one she'd made with his name on it. Her hand stilled mid-air.

Evan and Lindsey rounded the corner of the barn behind him. She couldn't look at him. Her damned eyes burned with unwanted moisture.

He stopped beside her and bent to kiss the top of her head. His hand settled at her back. "Got anything in there for me?"

She dug in the basket and shoved his favorite ham and cheese in his general direction. "I'll come back later and collect everything." She brushed past them. "It was nice to meet you, Lindsey."

"Shayna, wait," Evan called after her.

She pretended not to hear him as she entered the barn and ran smack dab into Bradi. "Sorry."

"Sorry about that," Bradi said at the same time and moved to one side. She looked past Shayna, a big grin spreading across her face. "Hi, Ev."

"Shit." Shayna took off again, swiping at the tears that rolled down her cheeks.

"Shayna, stop."

"I'm busy, Evan. Stuff to do." *Bags to pack. Miles to drive.* "And you have company."

She'd just stepped out of the barn when his fingers circled her upper arm, still tender from the night before. He spun her around. "Will you stop?"

Resigned, she stood still but stared at her dusty feet, refusing to let him see her cry. "What?"

"I'm sorry," he said simply. "I didn't know she was coming with Bradi, or I would have told her not to."

"No need to explain." Shayna blew out a shaky breath. "We both have pasts, and it's your house. You can invite anyone you want. Besides, I have stuff—"

"Dammit, Shay." He let go of her arm to frame her face with both hands. He tilted her head back, and his mouth slanted across hers. His tongue slid between her lips in a slow kiss that made her tummy flutter. Her nipples peaked, and she leaned into him, her hands fisting into his shirt.

Desire clouded her thoughts, almost making her forget why she'd been desperate to get away. Then he drew back, nipping at her lower lip.

He swept a thumb over her wet cheek. "I didn't ask her to come here. She rode along to keep Bradi company. End of story."

Whether he invited her or not wasn't the issue. The issue was he owed her nothing. He'd made no promises, and she'd gone into their agreement with her eyes wide open when she'd made her *I only want sex* spiel. That she'd changed her mind, wanting more, didn't mean he had.

Blinking back another rush of tears, she blew out another jerky breath and shook her head. "It doesn't matter."

"It does to me. I want you to understand there's nothing between me and Lindsey." He kissed her again, quick and hard. "We're just friends."

She looked into his eyes. "You and I both know you're more than friends."

"Okay, yes, I have—I've *had* a somewhat complicated relationship with her, and I care for her as a friend. But that's it."

Shayna wanted to believe him, and maybe he was telling the truth, but she'd already known their time together was limited to the ranch and Lindsey's presence only sped up the timeline. That left her with now…and tonight if she stayed. Would she let her jealousy take that away from her?

It just hurt so damn much.

She sniffed. "She's very beautiful."

"Is she?" He released her face but wrapped his arms around her to bring her in close. "I hadn't noticed."

She pushed against his chest. "Don't dismiss me like that."

"You're right." He loosened his hold but didn't let her go. "I'm sorry. She is attractive." He leaned in to whisper, "But she doesn't make me burn like you do."

Shivering, she masked his effect on her with a snort. "I wasn't fishing for a compliment. Just stating a fact."

"So am I." He nuzzled her ear. "Will you let me introduce you to both her and Bradi?"

"We met at the house." She angled her head to give him room to kiss the crook of her neck.

He lifted his head. "Please?"

The plea drew her gaze back to his face. Evan wasn't a man to beg. He demanded. He took. That he asked told her exactly how important Lindsey was to him, which almost hurt more than knowing their past.

One more night. Don't throw it away.

Still, her pride wouldn't let her give in too easily. "I'll play nice on one condition."

He tilted his head to one side. "Only one?"

"Maybe two if you're lucky." She slid her hand up the blue T-shirt stretched tight over his pecs.

His brow lifted. "Name your price."

She bit her lip and glanced up at him from under her lashes. "I want you to tie me up and give me multiple orgasms tonight."

His eyes flashed with heated promise. "And?"

She palmed the stubble starting to show on his jawline and gave him a teasing smile. "I'll let you decide the *and*."

With a groan, he tightened his hold and lowered his mouth to hover over hers. "Do you know how much I want to pin you against the barn and fuck you, right now?

The hard length pressing into her belly sent heat to her core. "I have some idea."

"Are you two gonna be done soon?" Josh asked from a few feet away, and Shayna nearly jumped out of her skin. "We could use some help in here."

A different heat flooded her cheeks as she focused on the group behind Josh in the barn. Bradi, Lindsey, and the guys stood waiting, all eyes on her and Evan. The two women shared a knowing glance and smile.

God, they'd been making out in the barnyard with an audience, and she'd been oblivious.

"Come on." Evan chuckled, and he unwound his arms from around her and clasped her hand in his. "Josh looks like he's about to explode."

Trying to focus on Evan and the fact he seemed unconcerned that they'd been caught practically humping each other, she let him lead her into the barn to meet his friends. She could do this. For Evan.

It wasn't like she'd ever see them again. Or Evan. Because tomorrow, when she left for her shift at the hospital, she wouldn't be coming back.

****

"I'm sorry I screwed things up for you and Shayna." Lindsey leaned against the wall as Evan settled the mare in her stall.

"You didn't." If anything, Lindsey's appearance had given Evan a glimpse of Shayna's feelings. Or at least he hoped the jealousy and hurt in her eyes were an indication of how she felt about him, that she wanted more than her original request for sex.

He closed the stall door and looked outside the barn to watch Shayna help Josh toward Bradi's truck.

"At least she's not glaring daggers at me anymore."

No, Shayna had actually made an effort to give Lindsey the benefit of the doubt. She'd been sweet and friendly through his introductions and accepted Lindsey's apology with grace.

And from his position during the procedure, he'd kept an eye on her as she sat between Josh and Lindsey. The two women seemed to chat amicably. Of course, Lindsey could charm the angriest customer at the bar she ran for her father.

"Is she the one who broke you?

He swung his gaze back to Lindsey "I don't really know what or who broke me, but she was the one who made me realize I was broken."

"Did you love her back then?"

That was an easy question, and Evan didn't hesitate to answer. "Yes."

She nodded. "Do you love her now?"

"I don't think I ever stopped." Saying it out loud only reaffirmed what he already knew.

"I thought so. I've never seen you smile this much or touch anyone intimately outside our sessions."

He shrugged. "Can't seem to help myself."

"I always wondered who might have hurt you." Uncrossing her booted feet, she straightened away from the stall. "There's usually a betrayal or something like it behind a man as commitment shy as you."

He shook his head. "She didn't hurt me. I hurt her."

"I see." Lindsey glanced at Shayna trying to help Josh in the truck. "You know she can't fix you, right?"

A grin split his face. "I don't think she wants to. She likes my broken parts." Then his smile faltered. "Some of them, anyway. I'm still not sure she'll like them all."

"Which parts won't she like?"

He debated telling her. He'd already revealed too much. But Lindsey had a way of seeing through people and situations to the heart of the matter. "She likes bondage and rough sex."

"Then you mean sharing?"

"I do."

"Are you going to take her to the dungeon?"

Evan took off his hat, wiped his brow with his sleeve, and set the hat back into place. "I thought about it, but it would take too long to get there and back, and she can't be up all night and leave tomorrow for her weekend shift at the hospital. I thought Tate might work out, but she'll have to get to know him first."

She stopped to look at him. "What's your hurry? Why not wait 'til next week?"

He sighed. "I haven't been…satisfied as a Dom lately."

She nodded. "Clay said as much and that it was a matter of time before we lost you."

Of course Clay would recognize Evan's need to take lead and the frustration building from the lack of control over a scene. "It's not just that. I can't tell her how I feel and give her hope only to have her unable to accept all of me. And after today, it's more important than ever that she know."

"Again, sorry about making a mess." Her smile brightened. "But I'm not sorry to see you happy. I'd much rather lose you to love than dissatisfaction."

Evan chuckled. "Never dissatisfied with you. Just needing more and wanting what you and

Clay have."

"You know," she said, turning to slowly stroll down the corridor of the barn, "she likes Josh's broken parts, too."

Evan's gut clenched as the jealousy he'd felt all week reared its head again. It had lessened some after talking to Shayna last night and a little more after seeing her reaction to Lindsey.

The only things broken about Josh were body parts. Did Lindsey see more between them than he did? "What do you mean?"

She rolled her eyes. "I don't mean she's in love with him, dumbass. That girl's got eyes for nobody but you. I just mean she's comfortable with him, and if you're going to introduce her to a threesome, he might be your guy."

"I don't think so." Everything in him balked at the idea. But as Shayna climbed in Bradi's truck to sit beside Josh in the back seat, he felt only a twinge of the jealousy he'd felt the last few days. And he hadn't even thought about them that way when she'd stuck close to Josh while he crooned Star during with the insemination. Only that he'd been glad Shayna had Josh to lean on emotionally as Lindsey chattered away.

Lindsey turned to walk backward as they left the barn and neared the truck. "Okay, I'm just saying."

"I'll think about it."

"Good, 'cause I'd really love to see you happy. You deserve it." Her voice lowered. "Though I'll miss you like crazy."

"I'll still be around." Though he really didn't want to think about the possibility of ever again being a third for Clay and Lindsey. That would mean things hadn't worked out with Shayna.

He glanced again at Shayna beside his brother. Her gaze locked with his, and he read her discomfort with his private conversation with Lindsey, but she looked away, her attention returning to Josh and something he said. She smiled, but it didn't reach her eyes. He had to cut this goodbye short.

Evan opened the truck door for Lindsey and moved to the rear window. He leaned in to brush his lips against Shayna's. "I'll be up later." He looked across the front seat. "Bradi, thanks for coming to our rescue."

"Anytime."

He backed away from the truck. "See ya, Lindz."

The truck rolled up the road to the house, and he swung around to head back to the barn. The guys were all busy with chores, and he aimed to pitch in. He always thought best when his hands were occupied.

And he had a lot to think about.

Chapter Eleven

While Josh napped in his recliner downstairs, Shayna had showered, wove her hair into a French braid, and put on a yellow sundress. Then she'd made dinner and ate with Josh in the front room. Or Josh had. Her stomach was in knots, so she'd only pushed the food around on her plate.

She'd finally saved a plate for Evan since he still hadn't returned from the barn. It was well after dark, which ramped up her nerves and left her wondering what his no-show meant. Was he avoiding her, his thoughts on what he could be doing to Lindsey? The conversation between the two had seemed intense, and they'd both looked a little sad when Lindsey left.

Everything in Shayna urged her to leave, too. Now. But like an addict, she had to have one more taste of him.

The squeak of the screen door startled her, and her heart lurched as Evan stepped into the kitchen. He hung his straw hat on the rack and stood staring at her, his eyes turbulent. His lips thinned, not in an angry way, but in a way that said he wanted to say something but couldn't form the words.

And that tore at her heart. Evan was a quiet man, but he never had trouble speaking his mind when he had something to say.

She took a step toward him and stopped. "Is everything all right?"

He ran both hands over his face and blew out a long breath. When he looked at her again, some of the stress around his eyes had disappeared. "I'm going up to shower."

"Don't you want to eat?"

"Maybe later." He turned and walked out of the room.

Shayna gripped the chair in front of her, more confused than before. *Run, you idiot. Get the hell out.*

Ignoring the voice of self-preservation, she drew a pitcher of hot water and headed to the front room to give Josh his last bath. The last one given by her, anyway.

Five minutes later, she had him sitting on the edge of the bed, a towel covering his lap, and was scrubbing his back. He'd been quiet all evening, and she'd been content to let him stay that way, but now…

"This is your last sponge bath." She washed the soap away. "You don't need me anymore."

"I knew it." He twisted to frown at her. "I

knew you'd let her drive you off."

She shook her head. "Lindsey being here just sped up the process of me leaving. I'd already made the decision to find another weekday job. Besides, you need a housekeeper, not a nurse."

"Don't put this on me. You're running."

"Maybe."

"There's no *maybe* to it." He turned away and sighed. "I thought you had more fight in you than that."

"Sometimes you have to cut your losses." She toweled him dry and climbed off the bed to kneel at his feet. She washed around the cast, then moved on to his other leg.

His finger tapped under her chin, forcing her to look at him. "He loves you."

"He hasn't said so." She pulled away to rinse him off. "And I can't wait around for him to leave me again. I won't survive it."

He didn't say anything else until she handed him the sponge to wash under the towel covering his privates. "This being my last bath and all, you could at least make it more fun."

Dragging a towel down his calf, she smiled, glad he wasn't going to make this harder than it was. "I'm sure Wendy and Brianne are all about the fun."

"Are you almost done?" Evan's smooth

baritone intruded from the door.

Josh's head snapped up, and Shayna jerked. How long had he been there? Had he heard her decision to leave?

"Almost," she said without looking at him.

She finished drying Josh before she glanced over her shoulder at Evan propped against the casing. His hair was still wet from his shower. He was shirtless, and his feet were bare. His jeans hugged his thighs and rode low on his hips. Her belly fluttered as she took in the outline of his erection. He was hard for her already.

Even as he stole her breath and made her panties wet, her heart ached. She should have listened to the voice in her head telling her to go. She might have one more night with him, but it would never be enough.

****

Evan crooked a finger at Shayna. "Come here."

His chest constricted, the rope around it coiling tighter, as he waited for her to follow his command. The sight of her kneeling before Josh was a double-edged sword. His brain told him not to go through with his plan, but his cock stretched behind his fly and the Dom in him fought for control.

Since Lindsey suggested inviting Josh to partner with him in a threesome with Shayna, he'd thought of nothing else. It made sense in a twisted way. She was comfortable with Josh and admitted they'd both been interested but nothing happened. The chemistry was already there. Enough to make her first attempt at a ménage easier. And he needed her to want it as much as he did.

For a minute, he didn't think she'd obey, but she rose on her bare feet and crossed the ten feet between them. When she stopped a few inches away and lifted her gaze to meet his, he caught the uncertainty in her eyes.

He brushed a stray hair from her face and kept his voice low, only for her ears. "Are you ready for your *and*?"

Desire mingled with uncertainty in those big brown eyes. "Yes."

Evan let go of his doubts. He couldn't go into this half-assed.

Placing his hands on her waist, he tugged her against him and lowered his head to taste her lips—mint and berries. He dipped deeper into the hot cavern of her mouth. Her tongue swirled around his without hesitation.

Groaning, he looped his arms around her middle to pull her flush against him from thigh to chest and deepened the kiss. He took his time exploring the hollow of her cheek, her teeth, under her tongue. His heart hammered at his ribs. His lungs strove for air. His dick strained against his fly.

Her arms snaked around his neck, fingers sifting through his hair. Her soft touch sent a shudder along his spine. He palmed her ass with both hands, lifted, and dragged her pussy against his cock for a fraction of relief. Her heat whispered through her dress and his jeans.

She whimpered into his mouth and wrapped one leg around his thigh to grind against him.

Easing one arm to the small of her back to hold her in place, he smoothed a hand along her side to fill it with her plump breast. He grazed the rigid bud with his thumb. She arched into his hand.

As he rolled her nipple between his thumb and index finger, he severed the kiss to whisper against her lips. "I need you."

"You have me," she murmured.

Trailing open-mouthed kisses along her cheek, he made his way to her ear. "Who do you belong to?"

She sighed. "You."

"That's right." He nipped at her earlobe, drawing a tremor of pleasure-pain from her. "You're mine. To do with as I please. And tonight, I want to share you."

He lifted his head and waited for his words to catch up to her lust-fueled brain. Waited for her decision to join him in his world…or shatter it.

Eyelids fluttering, she stared up at him, a myriad emotion playing across her face. Desire. Confusion. Understanding. Shock. Embarrassment.

She twisted to peer at Josh over her shoulder, then back at him. Interest lit her eyes, and finally, what he'd hoped for—desire—mingled with acceptance and anticipation.

The coil squeezing his chest loosened. *She wants it.*

Or does she just want Josh?

Before he let doubt change his mind, Evan slowly lowered the zipper of her dress. He eased the tiny straps from her shoulders, and the butter-colored cotton pooled at her feet, leaving her bare except for a pair of light blue lace panties. She shivered and placed her hands behind her back.

"Are you sure?" he asked, needing to hear the words.

Her chocolatey gaze met his. "I'm sure."

"Evan?" Josh's raspy voice drifted over their hushed conversation. "What's going on?"

He met Josh's wary gaze over the top of Shayna's head. "Either you want to join us, or you don't. Tell me now."

Swallowing hard, Josh studied him for a moment, confusion and lust battling behind his eyes. "Shayna?"

"Let's show him how much you want him." Evan lowered her to the floor, turned her to face Josh, and filled his hands with her breasts. He squeezed and kneaded and played with the beaded tips as he bent to nuzzle the skin beneath her ear. "He likes your tits."

She bit her lip, then let it slip free to a soft smile as she met Josh's gaze and thrust out her chest, her breasts rising in invitation.

The tent of Josh's towel rose higher, and his shoulders relaxed. The rope around Evan's chest loosened a bit more. Josh dropped his gaze to her breasts. That alone told Evan he was into the threesome they were offering.

Evan lifted both mounds and thumbed the taut peaks. "I've seen him stare at your breasts when you give him a bath and your nipples are pushing through your wet clothes. He wants to suck them, and I want to watch."

Head falling back to rest against his shoulder, she moaned and covered his hands with hers.

With a quick flip of his wrist, he captured hers in a tight grip and slowly lowered her arms behind her until her palms touched his thighs. "Keep your hands here. Do you understand?"

"Yes."

Gliding one hand up her arm to recapture a breast, Evan trailed the fingers of his other hand over her flat belly to the top of her panties. He stalled there, teasing along the tiny band above her mound. She trembled, and her breathing became shallow and quick. As he tunneled his fingers under her panties, her hips tilted to reach for them.

His middle finger glided between slick folds. The little nub between them was hard and swollen.

"Mmm, you like the idea of Josh sucking your tits, don't you?"

"Yes," she said on a breathy sigh. Her fingers dug into his thighs.

"I want to watch your face as he takes you into his mouth and sucks hard." He pinched her nipple and plunged his finger into her wet heat. A small cry escaped her parted lips. "But first I want to watch you suck his dick like you did Tucker's. Will you do that for me?"

Evan held his breath again, waiting for Shayna's reply. Every step of the way, he had to know she was doing this for herself and not just for him. It wouldn't work between them if she only complied to make him happy. She had to want it, too.

****

Her body humming with need, Shayna blinked and tried to think past Evan's touch and the pleasure building in her core. What was the question? Would she give Josh a blow job?

She looked at Josh. He'd removed the towel from his lap and was stroking his cock. Her inner muscles contracted around Evan's finger, and she licked her lips.

Having compared Josh to Evan many times in the past, she'd always felt physically drawn to him.

Now, she had no trouble separating the two. Tall like Evan, Josh's long legs were muscular but lean. His shoulders were a little broader, his chest slightly thicker from working the ranch day in and day out all his life. His hair was sun streaked while Evan's hair was more of a dirty blond. And his cock…not as thick as but slightly longer than Evan's.

She wasn't sure what the outcome of their actions tonight would be or how this would affect their friendship, but yes, she wanted Josh. And she wanted Evan to watch her suck Josh's dick like he'd watched her with Tucker. Nearly as much, she needed Josh, needed to cross the line they'd drawn in the proverbial sand. She wanted his hands on her body, his cock in her mouth. She wanted to fuck him.

Shayna lifted her gaze to Evan's, and her pulse quickened at the controlled heat gleaming in his steel blue eyes. Her hips jerked against the heel of his hand on her mound. Moisture trickled down her thighs. "I'll do whatever you ask."

His chest relaxed as a long breath whooshed from his lungs. Had he been worried she wouldn't? Silly man.

He lowered his lips to hers and kissed her deeply, thoroughly. His finger pistoned in and out, clouding her mind once again with his intoxicating touch. Her blood pulsed faster, louder in her ears. Pressure built in her core. She was close to orgasm.

But Evan eased out of the kiss as he slipped his finger from her soaked pussy and from under her panties. She moaned at the loss and squeezed her thighs together for relief.

"Mmm, sweet," Evan murmured.

Josh groaned, and she opened her eyes to see Evan sucking his finger. A shiver quaked through her.

He pulled the finger from his mouth. "Do you remember your safewords?"

Safewords? She hadn't needed them so far, and she trusted him not to hurt her in a non-pleasurable way. But to make him happy, she said the words he needed. "Traffic lights."

"Good girl." He stepped to one side and squatted next to his duffel bag by the doorway. She hadn't even noticed it. He withdrew a small box and opened it to reveal a short chain with clamps on each end. Rising, he said, "Hands behind your back."

Her nipples already tingling, she obeyed, and he bent to suck one tip into his mouth. He drew hard. Pain brought her to her toes, but she arched for him to take more as pleasure rippled from her breast to her core. He released her with a pop, then tugged the bud with his fingers to slip the clamp in place.

She inhaled sharply as the pinch sent another streak of pleasure-pain to her clit.

"Okay?" he asked.

Nodding, she bit her lower lip in anticipation of the next clamp. With the second clamp came exquisite torture. She shivered as the pain rolled through her.

Once it was in place, he gave the chain a tug.

"Ayah," she yelped at the needlelike sting.

"Beautiful." He trailed a finger from nipple to nipple. His gaze lifted to hers. "One more thing and we'll begin."

Digging through his magic bag again, Evan pulled out two condoms and tucked them into his back pocket.

"Does it hurt?" Josh asked.

She nodded. "I love it."

Butterflies swarmed in her belly as he openly caressed her with his gaze. This was really happening. Fucking two men… At the same time or separately? Numerous scenarios of a threesome played in her mind, and each aroused her more than the next.

Evan rose with a skein of blue rope, hesitated, then put it back in the duffel. When he stood again, blocking her view of Josh and essentially returning them to their little bubble of hushed conversation. He held out the wrist cuffs she was growing to love. "Hands in front."

"Not behind me?"

"Not this time." He clasped one around her wrist and thrust a thumb over his shoulder. "He won't be able to help you keep your balance, so I'll leave your hands bound in front but loose." He secured the second. "How's that?"

She turned them over and then back. "Good."

His lips thinned as he rubbed the sensitive skin at her wrists. "I'm sorry I can't give you all the restraint you need, but we'll make do."

Raising a cuffed hand, she palmed his cheek. "It's enough."

You're enough.

His jaw clenched beneath her fingers, and his Adam's apple bobbed. What were the words stuck in his craw? What couldn't he bring himself to say? Was the lack of restraint bothering him that much? Was it not enough for him?

He lowered her hand, circled behind her, and grasped her upper arms in that now familiar grip that made her heart race and her juices flow. With a gentle nudge of his hips, he walked her across the open space of wood flooring to the bed. He stopped just out of Josh's reach.

"You are mine," Evan said loud enough for Josh to hear. "You will only take instruction from me. If he tells or asks you to do something, you will look to me for permission. Is that clear?"

Shayna closed her eyes and bit her lip to focus pain somewhere other than her heart. He meant for tonight, for right now, but she'd always be his. "Yes."

"Shayna, are you sure you want to do this?" Evan asked.

Her eyes snapped open as she turned her head to look at him over her shoulder. Lust blazed in those steely-blue eyes. He wanted her. The reminder notched up her confidence and her desire to please him. Both him *and* Josh. "I'm sure."

He nodded and scooted her closer to the edge of the mattress, then tossed a throw pillow on the floor in front of Josh. With a slight pressure from his hand on her shoulder, she sank to her knees between Josh's legs. His cock bobbed and stretched another half inch. Thick veins wove the length of his shaft. Pre-cum leaked from the mushroomed head.

Her tummy fluttered, and saliva flooded her

mouth. Her heart took up a trot. All she had to do was bend slightly forward and she would taste him, but she knew to wait for instruction.

She peered up at Josh, and her breath caught in her throat. His blue eyes were like twin flames, luring her closer. Her clit twitched in anticipation of the burn.

Evan shifted into her peripheral view. "Take him into your mouth."

Mindful of Josh's cast, she braced a forearm against his right thigh and licked her lips to wet them.

Both men groaned.

She suppressed a smile as she opened her mouth and closed it around the head of Josh's cock. Wrapping the fingers of one hand around the base of his shaft, she reached with her other hand to tease the underside of his balls. At the same time, she swirled her tongue around the sensitive edge and over the slit.

Salty. Nice.

She ran her tongue down the length as far as it could reach.

"Fuck." Josh's hand landed on her head, not to guide or force her to do more. It was more of a caress. "So hot."

She darted a glance up to find Josh watching her, his gaze locked on her lips. Her clit twitched, and her pussy contracted, needing to be filled. She took him deeper, letting the spongy tip ride against the roof of her mouth as her tongue traced the vein on the underside of his shaft.

"Oh yeah." Josh flexed his hips, shoving his cock to the back of her throat.

In a natural rhythm, she worked up and down his iron length. Her breathing sawed in and out as she licked and sucked.

The sound of a zipper lowering drew her attention to Evan. He shoved his jeans down and stepped out of them. His hand curled around his thick erection. His balls drew tight against his body.

She let her gaze roam upward, over his pectorals and higher. His features were relaxed, but his eyes blazed with lust, and it was like reliving the night at the lake with Tucker. Heat flared in her core, and just like that night, she grew heady with the power she held over each man.

"Suck him harder." Evan's bourbon-rich voice rasped over her.

Concentrating on her task of giving both Evan and Josh pleasure, she squeezed Josh's cock with her cheeks and took long leisurely passes from base to tip. Her fingers around his shaft tightened and followed her mouth's journey up and down.

Josh hissed. "Fuck, that's… *Fuck.*"

Evan grunted his approval, and Josh's fingers

tightened in her hair. She sucked harder, determined to maintain control.

"That's it, Shay." Evan's voice floated from behind her. "Just like that."

Listening closely, Shayna tracked him to the bedside table. He placed the condom packets on top, then she lost him again.

A second later, his warmth enveloped her as he knelt behind her. An open-mouthed kiss wet the side of her neck, and his stiff cock tapped her spine. "Watching your mouth swallow his dick makes me hot…hard. I know exactly what he's feeling, how good you are."

Evan's fingers wandered around and up her ribs to tweak her nipples, and she moaned. In turn, Josh applied a pressure on her head. She didn't resist. She took him deeper.

Should she have? Evan hadn't given either of them permission to change the course he'd set. She didn't care. She'd suffer whatever punishment he administered and then some.

"He wants to come in your mouth," Evan whispered in her ear. "I want to see you swallow. Will you let him?"

His words were like fuel to the flame of her desire. She ached to have him inside her. In answer, she sucked harder and plunged faster, deeper, on Josh's cock. Her eyes watered. Saliva leaked and dribbled over her hand.

"Fuck, fuck, fuck." Josh stiffened, his hand fisting in her hair.

Spurts of cum hit the back of Shayna's throat. She swallowed quickly and continued to pump with her hand and mouth to prolong his pleasure as long as possible, until she'd consumed the last drop and his cock softened to semi-erect.

As she let Josh slip from her lips, he untangled his fingers from her hair and fell back on the bed, one arm slung over his eyes. "Jesus, you're good at that."

Evan eased her back to rest against his chest. He wiped her mouth and hands with Josh's towel. "Are you okay?"

"I need you inside me." She squirmed to find relief, her breath whooshing in and out. "I need to come."

"Soon." He kissed her forehead. "First, I want to feel your hot lips around my dick. Do you need a minute?"

"No, I'm ready," she said, eager to please him, to give him what he needed. Then maybe—no, not maybe. He *would* give her what she ached for.

"Good girl." He dangled a two-inch chain in front of her, then drew her hands behind her back to connect the cuffs. "For *our* pleasure."

He rose to stand beside her, and she pivoted to face him, aware of Josh's cast behind her and his other knee close to her breast, the crisp hair on his leg tickling her skin. The broad head of Evan's cock bounced toward his belly button, then rested at an outward angle. Two bulging veins threaded the underside, and a pearlescent drop of fluid formed at the tip.

The backs of his knuckles grazed her cheek. "If you keep looking at me like that, I won't last long."

Her gaze flew upward, and she smiled. "Then I'd better make it worth your while…as long as that is."

For the first time since he'd entered the room, the corners of his mouth tipped up fully, and his eyes sparkled with humor. "I know it will be."

Moving closer, he rested the wet tip of his cock on her mouth. Instinctively, she parted her lips and swept her tongue over the spongy head. She closed her eyes as the salty essence of Evan rolled over her taste buds. "Mmmmmm."

The rustling of sheets drew her attention to the bed. Josh propped himself up on his good elbow, his gaze fixated on her mouth. Hunger blazed in those icy blue depths, triggering her need to give him as much of a show as she'd given Evan. She wanted Josh on the razor-sharp edge of ravenous.

Her focus returned to Evan, and she opened her mouth as he guided his bulbous crown between her lips. She sucked in an inch and ran her tongue around his shaft. Her eyelids fluttered shut, and she slid farther down his length.

"That's it. Suck me hard." He rocked back and plunged in again as she hollowed her cheeks. Framing her face with splayed palms, he angled her head and drove to the back of her throat.

She tried to breathe between his deliberately slow thrusts. Working him with her tongue, she found a rhythm to match his. She ached to touch him, to feel her way over his hardened muscles and grip his sculpted ass, but the ache of restraint was a sweeter torment.

"You look good on your knees." His words were rough, gravelly.

She opened her eyes and found him watching her closely, his breathing as labored as hers.

He stroked a thumb at the corner of her mouth. "I love fucking your mouth. So good. So hot…wet."

Josh sat up. His finger teased her shoulder, sending a tremor to her breast. Blood surged to her nipple eliciting a delectable sting.

"She likes this…us watching," Evan said to Josh without looking at him. "I'll bet her pussy is as juicy as her mouth."

Yes. Yes, it is.

Josh growled.

"If you were able, you could check." Evan's

tongue slid along his lower lip. "Or maybe fuck her from behind."

"I wish I could." Josh fisted his revived cock and stroked along with their pace. "Fucking cast."

Shayna whimpered as thoughts of Josh slamming into her pussy while she sucked Evan off played in vivid color in her mind.

"It wouldn't take much to make her come." Evan's eyes narrowed on her. "But you won't. Not yet."

She hummed her understanding. He grunted and pumped faster. She quickened her tongue action and increased the suction. That was all it took.

He threw back his head. A guttural cry tore from his lips. His hips jerked, and cum shot into her mouth. She drank him down, savoring the taste of Evan. He held her still, but she kept milking the way he liked.

A long moment later, he withdrew but kept her face firmly in his hands. She fought for air. Sweat dampened the back of her neck under her braid and trickled down her spine. She kept her gaze locked on his face, enjoying his sated expression, knowing she put it there.

When he finally lowered his head and met her gaze, her heart soared. Pride and something else stirred in his eyes. Happiness? Admiration? Love? Dare she hope? Whatever it was vanished, and the fire of dark lust returned.

"You're amazing." He smiled. "You deserve a reward."

White-hot desire unfurled from her center outward, searing her senses. She didn't know what he had in store for her, but she trusted him and was certain she wanted it as much as he did. Maybe more.

Chapter Twelve

Evan held Shayna's head in his hands, her face flushed with need. Her breath rushed in and out between her swollen lips. Her seductive dark eyes hid behind heavy lids, thick black lashes weighing them down.

The tightness around Evan's chest had all but released him. She had surpassed his expectations, taken all he'd demanded, and the cream soaking her panties said she was prepared for more.

He wished her hands and ankles were cuffed and tied to each corner of the bed. He wanted her spread eagle and at his mercy. But Josh couldn't do the work he'd come to rely on from Clay or his other dominant partners.

That aside, Evan was back in control, in his element. He felt freer and more alive than he had in months. Every step she took into his world chipped away at his doubt that she could be what he needed and unleashed a little more of the Dom inside him fighting to get out.

He inhaled deeply, and the scent of her juices filled his head. His cock filled with blood. As he drew in another breath, his spine tingled. He wanted to lay her across the bed, hold her down, and drive balls deep into her welcoming sheath.

Instead, he reached under her arms and hauled her to her feet. He turned her to face Josh. "I promised I'd let him suck your tits." He said to Josh, "It's her reward."

Josh licked his lips as he stared at her breasts. "Exquisite."

Evan stepped behind her and wrapped his fingers around her upper arms. He drew them back until her elbows grazed his ribs. The lush mounds rose higher. "Go ahead. Touch her."

Josh darted a glance from Evan to Shayna, then tentatively lifted his good hand to cup her breast.

A sigh slipped past her lips, and the sound shimmied over Evan and into his balls. He let go of one arm and smoothed a hand over her shoulder. Hooking an index finger under the chain linking the nipple clamps, he gave it a slight tug.

"*Ayah*," she shrieked and squirmed, her ass rubbing his erection. Her breathing fell into quick, jerky pants. "Oh sweet, freakin' hell, that hurt…so good."

He smiled and motioned to Josh. "Remove the clamps one at a time. When you do, her nipple will fill with blood and it'll sting. You'll need to suck hard to give her the pleasure to go with the pain. Think you can do that?"

"Fuck, Ev." Josh blew out a long breath. "I didn't know it could be good like this."

"I know." Another rope slipped from around Evan's chest. Josh had been so quiet that Evan hadn't been sure he would follow through to the end. It felt good to know his brother might actually understand him a little better now. But this wasn't the time to analyze Josh's acceptance of his brand of kink. "Just wait. It gets better."

With a shaking hand, Josh squeezed the clamp open. Shayna cried out, and he leaned in to cover her tit with his mouth. Her cry rounded into a moan as Josh sucked.

Evan growled and couldn't stop himself from sliding his dick between her legs. He groaned as his cock met with her warm, slippery folds.

"Jesus, Shay." He wanted to praise her, but his throat closed around the emotion building inside him. This was what he'd hoped for, dreamed of. Everything he'd ever wanted was within his grasp.

Josh released her breast, dragging her nipple through his teeth.

Another cry tore from Shayna, echoing in his ears, competing with his drumming heartbeat.

Needing to give her what she craved, Evan ran his fingers over the soft plane of her belly to her lace panties. Tunneling under the elastic, he eased his middle finger through the strip of saturated curls to find her swollen clit. He stilled, waiting for Josh to remove the second clamp.

The second her nipple was free and Josh took her into his mouth, Evan stroked the pouting button. "Come for me, Shay."

Her lips parted, but her scream of ecstasy was silent. Her hips bucked. Josh slipped his arm around her and yanked her against his chest as he continued to ravish her breast. Evan closed in from the rear, sandwiching her between them, holding her up when her knees buckled.

He nuzzled the hair at her temple. "So beautiful."

"Yes, she is." Josh licked and nipped the taut bud. "One of a kind."

Evan's nostrils flared as the scent of her juices surrounded him. He slowed the circular motion of his finger. Her breathing slowed, and her muscles relaxed as the orgasm they'd both given her waned. "Did you like your reward?"

Her eyes fluttered open halfway. A smile tipped her lips. "That…was…freakin' fantastic."

"So are you." He kissed her cheek. "And there's more where that came from."

Josh ran his hand over the swell of her hip. "Thank god, 'cause I could pound fuckin' nails."

A spike of possessiveness speared Evan with its sharp blade, but the fiery hunger raging inside him melted away his jealousy. He needed this.

Needed to watch another man fill her pussy, to see the pleasure she derived from another man's cock.

He jerked his chin at Josh. "Move over and lie down."

Evan held Shayna against him as Josh struggled to a reclining position with pillows propping him up. Evan twisted a hand in her panties, and with a quick jerk, he ripped the delicate lace from her body. Her soft gasp shimmed straight to his balls.

He nuzzled her ear and whispered, "If you want to stop now, say your safeword, but if you want to fuck him, climb up on the bed and give him a ride."

****

Shayna's body still buzzed from the ecstasy Evan and Josh had just given her, but Evan's words stirred her need for more, for penetration, for a hard, rough fuck. She tilted her head to search his face. The same need burned in his eyes.

Heart pounding faster, she nodded. She sought Josh's gaze. His wicked grin sent another aftershock of pleasure to her clit.

Evan guided her to the edge of the bed. "Can you stand on your own?"

She nodded, but her legs wobbled as he released her. A second later, the chain connecting the cuffs gave and her hands were free.

His magical fingers rubbed the stiffness from

her arms before he placed them on her waist. "I've got you, but brace yourself on his chest as you straddle him."

She hesitated. Not from fear or lack of interest, but to take in the sight of the man in front of her. She'd bathed Josh. She'd seen him naked. Hell, she'd just given him a blow job. Still, there was something different about taking this next step, actually having sex with him.

Not that she hadn't thought about it. Many times.

She soaked in the contours of Josh's sculpted arms, his shoulders, his pectorals, and the crisp blond hair centered between them. Lower, his rock-hard abs roller-coastered their way to the V cut in his groin. Golden hair feathered from his belly button to the base of his stiff erection.

His cock flexed, and her gaze darted to his. His twinkle in his eyes had been replaced with the same burning intensity as Evan's. She swallowed, but her mouth was dry.

"Shay?" An edge of concern deepened Evan's voice. "Do you want to continue?"

She held Josh's gaze. "Yes."

He nodded, and Evan's fingers flexed on her hips. "Up you go then."

She placed a knee on the mattress at Josh's left hip and flattened her hands on his chest. His skin was smooth and hot beneath her palms. "I'll try not to hurt you."

He quirked a half-smile, moved his broken arm out of her way, and lifted his other hand to caress her upper breast. "That's my line, but I'm guessing you wouldn't mind a little pain."

The levity in Josh's voice eased some of her nervousness, but his touch sent her pulse racing.

He moved his hand to her shoulder for support. "Come on, sweetheart."

She nodded, and with Evan's help from behind, she swung her leg over Josh's hips, taking care not to put weight on his injured leg. She found her balance and started to lower herself.

Evan's grip tightened, halting her descent. She looked over her shoulder.

"Not yet." He shifted her so that, instead of impaling herself on Josh's cock, she settled at the base. His length nestled between her wet folds, his hardness mashing into her clit.

Evan let her go and stepped away. "Don't move."

Don't move? She glanced at Josh, and his strained frown said it all. Both of them needed to move.

Evan returned with something in his hand. She groaned when she realized what he held. Her anal muscles clenched.

He opened the container and laid the butt

plug she'd worn the night before on the bed along with lubricant. "Lean forward. Ass in the air."

Shayna obeyed, lying her upper body over Josh's torso. His dick rode her clit, and the hair on his chest teased her nipples. His fingers trailed over her back, down and up, again and again, soothing her. She closed her eyes as cold lube oozed between her crack and Evan's index finger spread it around her sphincter.

"In a normal scene, I'd be prepping you to take *me* and not the plug." His finger breached the ring of muscle to his first knuckle. "I'd fuck you here"—his finger slid deeper—"while Josh fucked your pussy."

She shuddered, then whimpered as Evan filled her ass with two fingers and scissored them. Arching her back, she thrust against his hand. "Yes, more."

"Jesus." Josh's voice rumbled under her. His cock jerked, poking her belly.

Opening her eyes, she caught a glimpse of Josh's tongue as it snaked between his lush lips to wet them. His breath fanned her face. She lifted slightly and rocked forward, dragging her clit along his velvety length. Her mouth brushed his, and her tummy fluttered. His tongue reached for hers.

A scorching sting crawled across her scalp as Evan tugged on her braid. "No kissing."

A tinge of disappointment rolled through her, but Shayna smiled around Josh's mouth. Evan wanted her to fuck Josh but didn't want her to kiss him. That made no sense…unless he was jealous. Did that mean he loved her as Josh insisted? Was that the elusive emotion she'd seen in his eyes? Or was he simply angry because he hadn't given her permission yet?

Shayna hated to give up Josh's kiss or the exquisite prickling of her scalp, but with a sigh, she rocked backward onto Evan's fingers again. At the renewed friction of Josh's shaft rubbing her clit, cream trickled from her slit.

Evan removed his fingers, leaving her empty, but the rough pad of his scorching tongue lapped up her thigh to her opening. "Damn, I want to eat you."

Smack! The flat of his hand met her ass cheek.

"Ouch!" But she wiggled her ass for another swat. "What was that for?"

"For tempting me from my plan," he grumbled. "Naughty girl."

She didn't have time to tell him it wasn't her fault because he hadn't let her in on his plan as the tip of the plug centered on her anus. The toy glided in one smooth plunge until the flange met the resistant ring of muscle. Warmth blossomed in her ass and made its way to her core, prompting her to grind into Josh.

Smack!

"Don't move." Evan and Josh spoke together.

Josh's hand on her back lowered to squeeze the cheek Evan had spanked and hold her still. His chest rose and fell as he let out a long breath. "I want to be inside you when I come."

"Safety first." Evan took hold of her shoulders and eased her upright and slightly back on Josh's thighs. He opened the packet for Josh and handed him the condom.

"I can do it." Shayna reached for the condom, but Evan caught her wrist.

"He'll do it because I told him to." His tone was harsh but not angry. "And you'll wait for instruction, or there will be punishment." His voice softened. "I don't want tonight to be about that. I want you to have all the pleasure we can give you."

She wanted that, too. "I'm sorry."

He rubbed the skin he'd gripped, then tucked her hands against her chest to make room for Josh to roll on the condom. The sight of the latex sheathing his long cock had her squirming to do the same.

Evan stood back, his thick cock in hand. "Ride him."

Rising on her knees, she positioned over Josh. The ruddy crown probed her opening. She licked her lips and sank inch by slow inch, the wide girth stretching her inner walls. The fit was tight with the plug, but she closed her eyes and waited for her body to adjust.

Josh let out a long groan. His hand settled on her hip.

She took it as a sign he needed her to move. Lifting her lids, she slanted a look at Evan, waiting for permission, though he'd already told her to ride Josh.

His nod was slight but affirmative.

Eyes locked with his, she braced her hands on Josh's chest and rose, savoring the friction as she withdrew until only the head remained inside her slick channel. A tilt of her hips and she slammed home.

Evan's gaze lowered to where her body joined Josh's on the upward glide and downward plunge. She kept the same rhythm on the next rise and fall. Evan stroked his dick to her pace. Her breathing matched his.

"Fuck him hard." He jerked his dick. "Like you want it. Rough."

Shayna increased her pace. Josh's hand at her waist helped her. Pleasure threaded through her limbs, a river of fire.

"Look at him, Shay." Evan had moved closer. "He loves your pussy."

Josh thrust to meet her next downward slide. "Fuck me, Shay."

Shayna blinked as the flames spread from her pussy, warming her all over. Josh's sun-streaked hair fell over his forehead to cover one brow. His jaw was clenched tight. His gaze roamed from her face to her breasts, pausing there for a long moment, before moving on to her sex. Then it made the return trip to her mouth.

Moisture beaded her upper lip. She licked it away and renewed her efforts, undulating her hips. She explored the sculpted hills and valleys of his chest.

Josh bucked beneath her.

More sweat trickled down her spine and coated her thighs, mixing with her juices. Tingling sensations swirled in her core. Her muscles tightened. *So close.*

The other side of the mattress dipped, and something grazed her breast. Evan.

She'd been so caught up that she hadn't seen him move around the bed. He knelt behind but to one side of her, one leg between Josh's.

"I love watching you fuck." He coiled her braid in his fist and pulled, but only enough to promise the sting she wanted. "How your cunt sucks his cock."

Her inner walls contracted.

Josh grunted.

Evan snaked an arm around her waist, his fingers teasing over her belly. "Does he feel good inside you?"

"Yes."

"Do you want to come?"

"Yes…please."

"Good girl." His finger centered on her clit and rubbed in a circular motion. "Let go."

Ecstasy unfurled in her core, and she arched into the spasms of her orgasm. Her pussy clutched Josh's cock like a vise. A long moan ripped from her throat as pleasure raced along her nerve endings.

"Holy fuck…yes!" Josh's fingers bit into her hip as his release hit him. His shaft throbbed inside her as he filled the condom.

"Beautiful." Evan's low whisper rumbled beneath the drumming of her heartbeat.

Josh's body went slack beneath her. Except for the accelerated rise and fall of his chest he lay still.

The euphoric pulsing in her sex had barely waned when she felt herself lifted off Josh and placed on the bed beside him. Her breathing slowed, but she squeezed her legs together and wriggled her hips, savoring the tiny aftershocks.

Something soft clasped around her ankles, then her thighs. Lifting her head, she peered through heavy lids. Evan was buckling the last of the leather cuffs. He tucked her heels up close to her bottom and attached the ankle cuffs to the thigh cuffs with three-inch-long chains.

She tested the restraints and shivered at her immobility. He knew just what her body craved. If only he could read her heart. The thought stirred longings that had no place in this moment.

"Put your hands above your head." The command sounded rusty, as if his control had reached its limit. But he waited patiently for her to fling her heavy, spaghetti arms over her head before he addressed Josh, "Grab the chain and don't let go."

Strong fingers grasped the restraint between the wrist cuffs and pulled, stretching her arms taut as if he'd been into bondage all along. Mmm, delicious.

Evan palmed her knees and spread her legs wide. His fingers skimmed over her inner thighs to her center but fell away as he rose to his knees and loomed over her.

"Perfect." The icy-hot glint in his eyes stirred the coals of need simmering low in her belly. "You're mine now."

Swallowing the lump that suddenly formed in her throat, she returned his heated stare and nodded. She'd always been his. Always would be. "I'm all yours."

Whether you want me or not.

****

The tether on Evan's control was unravelling.

Watching Shayna come apart as she rode Josh and her climax to completion had him chomping at the bit to get inside her, to fuck her hard, to give her everything she needed. Seeing the love in her eyes that she tried to hide made him ache down to his very soul to give her everything he had, everything he was.

He couldn't walk away from her now if he tried, whether she accepted him or not. But she had. She'd encouraged his dominant side, urged him to take what he wanted, do what he wanted, and then she'd offered more.

Rolling a condom over his straining dick, Evan sucked in a long, calming breath and let it out. He covered her body with his, her soft, pale curves fitting perfectly under his hard, bronzed ones. His hips settled between her thighs, and he nudged the hot, slick entrance of her welcoming pussy with the head of his pulsing cock.

He feathered light kisses along her jaw and nipped at her bottom lip, puffy from stretching over his and Josh's dicks. Damn, she was beautiful.

Needing to claim her, he slammed into her welcoming heat. *Mine.*

She cried out, and he held still. *Mine.*

Evan slanted his mouth over hers and slipped his tongue between her parted lips, teeth clashing. *Mine.*

Her tongue danced around his, stroking it as she had his cock. He groaned and ground his hips into hers. She tried to meet his thrust, but he captured her hip with one hand and held her down. The cuffs kept her from using her feet as leverage. She was at his mercy.

Just as she'd been that night nine years ago.

Memories meshed with reality. They'd been perfect together then, and they were perfect together now. He needed her as desperately as she needed him.

Evan deepened the kiss and flexed his hips, beginning a punishing parry and thrust. His balls slapped against the plug in her ass. She moaned into his mouth, and her entire body went lax, revealing her trust in him.

Her surrender took him to the edge much quicker than expected. His balls drew tight to his body. He tore his lips from hers and buried his face in the crook of her neck as he rammed into her sweet cunt over and over.

"Come around me, Shay," he whispered. "Cover my cock with your cum. Let me feel you squeezing my dick."

"Close." Her breathy pants spurred him on, harder, faster.

He reached under her shoulder and felt for her braid. Wrapping it around his hand, he gave a slow, easy tug and dug the fingers of his other hand into the flesh at her hip.

"Ahh," she keened as her body stiffened and her sex fisted around him like a silk glove.

He arched, his hips locking as pleasure ripped through him in pulsing waves, dragging him under, stealing his breath. Her inner walls spasmed, milking ribbons of hot cum from his shaft as they rode the crashing waves together.

When his breathing slowed and his mind cleared, he braced his weight on his forearms and lowered his head to feather his lips over the shell of her ear. "I love you."

Her whole body stiffened beneath him. He lifted his head and zeroed in on the tears leaking from the corners of her closed eyes.

Fuck. Had he read her wrong? Did she not love him? He swallowed. "Shay?"

She shook her head. "Please don't say that unless you mean it. I can't—"

"I do mean it." He wiped her tears with his thumbs. "I love you."

Her eyes fluttered open, her dark eyelashes wet, her lower lip trembling. "You do?"

After everything he'd done wrong, both in the past and this week, he hoped she could forgive him, that she could love him. God knew he didn't deserve her. But his heart was hers. "I've never stopped loving you."

Sniffling, she gave him a watery smile. "Good, because I love you, too. I always have."

The breath he'd been holding rushed from his lungs. The tension in his gut eased. He lowered his head to taste her sweet lips.

"It's about damn time." Josh's voice startled them both.

Shayna laughed into his mouth, but Evan ignored him. "I'm sorry for everything I did to hurt you. I never should have left. I should have talked to you. We could have figured all this out together, and we'd be in an entirely different place right now."

"No, things are the way they had to be, like you said." She nipped at his lower lip. "And I kind of like where we are right now."

Evan caught movement above her head. Josh wasn't holding the chain. He was holding Shayna's hand. Oddly, his gut didn't tighten as it had before they started this scene. She loved *him* not Josh. She'd said the words. He believed her.

"If you two are through with all the fun and you're moving on to the mushy stuff, do you mind doing it upstairs." Josh let go of Shayna's hand to cover a yawn. "A guy's gotta get his beauty sleep, ya know."

Soft, melodic laughter drifted over Evan, stirring his semi-erect cock. Fuck, he wanted her again, wanted to make long, slow love to her, but she needed rest and aftercare.

Pulling out of her warm, velvety sheath, he rose to his knees and unbuckled the cuffs. She shuddered, then sighed as he removed the plug. He left the bed only long enough to wrap it and the condom in Josh's towel, then returned to scoop her off the bed.

Evan reached the doorway with Shayna in his arms and turned back to his brother. If not for Josh, he would never have found her again. "Thank you…for everything."

Josh nodded. "I love you, Ev."

"I love you, too, man."

"Take care of her."

"I plan to." He jutted his chin at the cuffs on the bed. "I'll come clean up later."

His brother picked up a cuff to examine it, interest sparking in his eyes. "No problem."

Smiling, Evan headed up the stairs. He had the woman he loved in his arms, and his brother was discovering the appeal of kink.

Shayna roused as Evan carried her past her door, her dark eyes wide. "Where are we going?"

"My room. To my bed." He didn't turn on the light as he crossed the room and stopped next to the bed. "This is where you belong." He lowered her feet to the floor and yanked back the covers. "You'll never sleep anywhere else if I have my way."

"I'm good with that." She yawned and crawled onto the mattress. Lying on her side, she patted the space beside her.

His dick strained in her direction, but he reined in his lust. "Aftercare first."

He turned to get his bag, but she rolled toward him and captured his hand. "I'm fine, really. I just want you to hold me."

Ignoring his instinct as a Dom, he caved to her plea and his own need to wrap himself around her. "Just for a minute."

Sliding in beside her, Evan lay on his back and drew her close, her head on his chest, their legs tangled. It wasn't just a matter of where she belonged. He was meant to be here, at her side. A rush of emotion had him grasping her hand in his. He brought it to his lips, his throat tight.

"Ev?"

He swallowed the lump in his throat. "Hmm?"

She lifted her head to look at him, her beautiful face veiled in moonlight shining through the open curtains. Her lashes lowered, then lifted, revealing all the love she'd been trying to hide over the last few days, more love than he ever imagined. She bit her lip, hesitating.

Letting go of her hand, he cupped her face and tugged her lip free of her teeth with his thumb.

"Tell me."

"Can we do it again?"

He groaned, and his control wavered. Lifting his head, he brushed his lips across hers. "I want to, believe me"—his head dropped to the pillow—"but I don't want to hurt you." She started to speak, but he pressed a finger to her gorgeous mouth. "I know, you're fine. But I have a responsibility to—

Her giggle vibrated through him.

"What's so funny?"

She curled her fingers around his wrist and dragged his finger from her lips. "I'm not that sore, but that's not what I meant."

"Tell me what you want." Anything. He'd give her anything.

"You…me…Josh."

A faint hint of jealousy stirred, but Evan shoved it back down. "Is that what you want? To be with Josh again?"

Her finely arched brows lifted, and she tilted her head. "I want *us* to be with Josh. I want—like—knowing you're watching and getting all hot. I want to give you what you want, and I…"

"Liked fucking him."

"Yes." She ducked her head. "I did."

Shit. He tipped her chin with his finger until she met his gaze. "Don't you ever feel guilty for enjoying a scene. I don't care who we're with. Whether it's Josh or not, I wouldn't have it any other way. Of course, it's up to Josh, though I'm sure he'll be happy to oblige."

He winced at the sarcasm of his last words, but she laughed and settled back into his arms. "I think so, too."

He hated to push, but he couldn't help himself. "What if he doesn't? Would you accept another partner?"

"Hmm, are you thinking about asking Tucker?" Her tone sounded skeptical and little scared. "Because you should know, he married Julie and they have five kids. And he's not as attractive as he used to be."

A bark of laughter burst forth before he could stop it. She was beyond priceless. "No, darlin', I wouldn't dream of asking Tucker. But I do have a partner in mind for us, for when you're ready."

She was quiet for a long moment, then propped her chin on his chest and batted her lashes at him. "Will you let him tie me up?"

Images of Shayna cuffed and tied up, of Tate eating her pussy flirted with his cock. *She* was flirting with danger. He suspected she knew that, but he was willing to see where she'd go, what fantasies she'd reveal. "Yes."

Her finger teased circles around his distended nipple. "Will you get hard watching him fuck my mouth?"

Blood pumped faster through his veins, and air rushed in and out of his lungs. "Yes."

She licked his nipple and bit it hard. "What else will you let him do to me?"

With a growl, he rolled her to her back and thrust his throbbing cock into her hot, wet vise. He reveled in the hiss of pain she sucked through her teeth. He gripped her wrists beside her head and captured her lower lip in a sharp bite. "How about I show you?"

Her inner walls flexed. She arched into him, then relaxed in surrender. "Mmm, yes, please."

"God, I love you." He licked the inside of her lip to ease the sting of his bite, then kissed her softly. "Say it. Say the words."

"I love you, Evan McNamara."

Evan closed his eyes as the last rope around his chest fell away. Shayna was his.

Epilogue

Evan couldn't take his eyes off Shayna…or his hands.

He skimmed his fingers over her silky skin where her backless teal dress dipped low to the base of her spine. He itched to peel it from her body and kiss every inch as he went. He'd thought about it all night.

She leaned into him. "She's beautiful."

He cast a quick glance at Lindsey and Clay as they took the floor for their first dance as husband and wife, then nuzzled Shayna's cheek. "Yes, you are."

Her brown eyes rolled upward. "Would you stop?"

"I can't." He sat back. "You're the only woman in the room as far as I'm concerned."

Her hand slid along his thigh. "And don't you forget it."

"Never." He'd wasted too much of his life without her. He'd be damned if he wasted another moment not showing her how much he loved her.

In the last three months, they'd struggled to

make a long-distance relationship work with her weekend shifts in Austin and his weekday schedule in Houston. He'd been on the verge of asking his partner to buy him out so he could move to Austin when she'd lowered her menu one night at dinner and told him she'd been offered a job at a hospital in Houston. She'd been quick to add that if he wasn't ready to take their relationship to the next level, she would turn it down.

He'd taken the key to his condo off his keyring and handed it to her right then and there. She had sublet her apartment the next day, given her two weeks' notice, and moved in with him.

"Where are they going for their honeymoon?" she asked.

Before he could answer, Bradi piped up from the other side of the table where she sat on Mason Montgomery's lap. "Punta Cana."

Shayna nodded. "Where are you two going?"

"We haven't decided," Bradi said, tugging on the sleeve of her silver bridesmaid dress, "but the wedding is still a long way off. Besides, we really can't leave the ranch."

Mason bounced her on his knee to get her attention. "We can go anywhere you want."

Bradi smiled and caressed his face. Light glinted off her engagement ring. "I know, but *you* know I'm too practical to get hung up on those things."

Evan thought about the ring in his pocket and how he'd planned to propose to Shayna tonight when they were alone. They'd already had a collaring ceremony. To him that meant forever, but her family expected a wedding, and she liked making her mother happy. He liked making Shayna happy.

Bradi shifted toward Evan. "Whatever we do, though, you two are invited." She looked at Shayna. "If it weren't for Evan, we wouldn't be together."

Shayna arched a brow. "Is that so?"

Mason frowned. "I'd like to think I'd have come around on my own."

"Eventually." Bradi smirked. "After I left town."

"Hmph." Mason lifted a brow. "Someone's asking for a spanking."

Bradi pressed her breasts against Mason's chest. "I can beg if you want."

With a growl, Mason lifted his fiancée to her feet and stood. "If you'll excuse us."

Laughing, Bradi wiggled her eyes at Shayna. "We'll be back."

When they were alone, Shayna turned her attention back to Clay and Lindsey. "They'll make really pretty babies."

Evan chuckled. Her new position at the Houston hospital had landed her in the nursery until a spot in the ER opened up. She didn't seem to mind.

"What?" She tilted her head to look at him. "You don't think they're a beautiful couple?"

"I think they're gorgeous." He grinned. "Maybe I can talk them into a foursome."

She snorted, then a smug smile lifted the corners of her mouth. "I wouldn't mind riding a fine specimen of a cowboy like Clay while you watch."

He groaned, and his cock tried to climb out of his cummerbund as the image of Shayna straddling Clay filled his mind. She'd adjusted well to the lifestyle Evan lived. They had enjoyed their time at the ranch with Josh, but as soon as his casts were off, Evan returned to work, and he'd introduced her to Tate Albrand. After a short time getting to know Tate, she'd accepted him, and he'd become their third on a regular basis at Silver House.

They'd also even seen Josh there a few times, dipping his toe into BDSM waters. He'd wanted to experiment at a club known to Evan, but he'd since mentioned finding a dungeon closer to Austin.

Shayna shook her head. "I've come to really like Lindsey, but my ego nor my heart would survive watching you with her."

"I don't want anyone but you, Shay." Trying to lighten the mood again, he said, "But if you want to go to the dungeon later, I'll tie you up and watch you and Tate."

A tremor shimmied through her, but she glanced at Clay and Lindsey dancing and sighed. "No, they've put me in the mood for romance. Can we just stay home?"

Evan frowned. "Are you tired of Tate?"

"You know I'm not, but honestly, Ev, as much as I love our time at the club and with Tate, you're all I'll ever need."

His heart expanded in his chest. God, he loved this woman. Still, he was glad she wasn't bored with Tate. There were only a handful of men at Silver House he'd let near her.

Tightening his arm around her, he kissed her forehead. "Can I still tie you up?"

"Of course." Her hand skimmed to the top of his thigh, and she peered at him from under her lashes. "I always want to be at the end of your rope."

Thank you for reading *End of His Rope*. I hope you enjoyed it. Watch for information about Josh's story in my newsletter.

https://www.darahlace.com/contact-darah/

About Darah Lace…

Born and raised in Texas, Darah Lace enjoys a crazy life with her husband and two dogs. She loves sports, music, reading/watching a good romance and penning scenes that sizzle. She prefers a hero who demands that ultimate satisfaction and a heroine who isn't afraid to explore her sexual fantasies. The author of erotic contemporary romance, Darah will lead you on a journey of desire, seduction, and forbidden pleasure.

Darah would love to hear from you.
Connect with Darah at

darah@darahlace.com
www.darahlace.com
www.facebook.com/darahlace
www.facebook.com/DarahLaceAuthor
www.instagram.com/darahlace/
www.linktr.ee/darahlace
TikTok @Darah_Lace_Author
Twitter @darahlace
Newsletter: www.darahlace.com/contact-darah/

Coming Soon

Taming the Wildcat

Cowboy Rough Book Four

By Darah Lace

Rancher Josh McNamara has two problems—rustlers keep cutting his fences and stealing his cattle and he can't stop thinking about the mysterious woman he'd shared last weekend. She'd been a wildcat in his arms and lit a fire in his gut for more, then disappeared before he learned her name. Hopefully, he'd solve one problem, with the help of the new sheriff in town.

Harper Quinn is hoping to leave her disastrous life behind and start fresh. A new job as sheriff of a small county where no one knows her past and there's no man to complicate her life. She's even found a new playground for when the urge strikes without the complications of a relationship. But when her first case involves the steamy cowboy she'd sunk her claws into last Saturday night, she begins to think she has the Midas touch when it comes to trouble.

Also Available

S.A.M.: Satisfaction Guaranteed

By Darah Lace

Hot off the assembly line, he's the perfect man.
Too bad he isn't real…or is he?

As the CEO of one of NYC's top ad agencies, Emma Raines devotes her time to stomping the competition in five-inch heels. She has no time for a love life, and her sex life is limited to a quarterly hook-up with a west coast colleague. When her pent-up desire sends her to the discreet offices of Weston Inc., one glance at a picture of SAM—their newest Sexually Animated Male—and she's dying for a taste of the more lifelike toy.

Sam Weston might be the genius behind the biomechanics of Weston, Inc., but the unexplained return of male sexbots by female customers has him scratching his head. When his cousin and co-founder cajoles him into a harebrained scheme to replace Emma's order with himself, the nerd in Sam is convinced research outweighs deception. The Dom in him scoffs at the idea of normal sex. But after one night of substandard vanilla, he's determined to take control and give the feisty exec the dominance she craves.

Other Books by Darah Lace

COWBOY ROUGH SERIES

Saddle Broke
Bucking Hard
End of His Rope
Taming the Wildcat (Coming Soon)

PRESTON BROTHERS SERIES

Bachelor Unmasked
Bachelor Auction
Bachelor Playboy (Coming Soon)
Bachelor Betrayed (Coming Soon)

STAND ALONES

S.A.M.: Satisfaction Guaranteed
Getting Lucky in London
Dragon's Bride
Sexting Texas
Yes, Master
Game Night
Wrong Number, Right Man
Yesterday's Desire

Printed in Great Britain
by Amazon